AM FIC

KU-304-409

Fiction Gift Aid
£

0 029310 041541

Chrysalis

Chrysalis

Anna Metcalfe

GRANTA

Granta Publications, 12 Addison Avenue, London W11 4QR
First published in Great Britain by Granta Books, 2023

Copyright © Anna Metcalfe, 2023

Anna Metcalfe has asserted her moral right
under the Copyright, Designs and Patents Act, 1988,
to be identified as the author of this work.

Quotation from 'On Transformation'
by Vladimir Nabokov, copyright © 2000, Vladimir Nabokov,
used by permission of The Wylie Agency (UK) Limited.

All rights reserved.
This book is copyright material and must not be
copied, reproduced, transferred, distributed, leased, licensed
or publicly performed or used in any way except as specifically
permitted in writing by the publisher, as allowed under the terms
and conditions under which it was purchased or as strictly permitted
by applicable copyright law. Any unauthorized distribution
or use of this text may be a direct infringement of the
author's and publisher's rights, and those responsible
may be liable in law accordingly.

*This book is a work of fiction. Any references to historical
events, real people or real places are used fictitiously.
Other names, characters, places and events are products of the
author's imagination, and any resemblance to actual events or
places or persons, living or dead, is entirely coincidental.*

A CIP catalogue record for this book
is available from the British Library.

1 3 5 7 9 10 8 6 4 2

ISBN 978 1 78378 908 5
EISBN 978 1 78378 909 2

Typeset in Garamond by M Rules
Printed and bound by CPI Group (UK) Ltd, Croydon, CR0 4YY

The pupa splits as the caterpillar had split – it is really a last glorified moult, and the butterfly creeps out – and in its turn hangs down from the twig to dry. She is not handsome at first. She is very damp and bedraggled. But those limp implements of hers that she has disengaged, gradually dry, distend, the veins branch and harden – and in twenty minutes or so she is ready to fly. You have noticed that the caterpillar is a *he*, the pupa an *it*, and the butterfly a *she*. You will ask – what is the feeling of hatching? Oh, no doubt, there is a rush of panic to the head, a thrill of breathless and strange sensation, but then the eyes see, in a flow of sunshine, the butterfly sees the world, the large and awful face of the gaping entomologist.

VLADIMIR NABOKOV

Contents

I

ELLIOT

One

I liked watching her. At first, she didn't notice or she didn't care. She never had that thing some people do where if someone's looking at them they feel it – a warm spot on the face or the neck – and then, without thinking, they turn. If she did feel the spot, she could ignore it. She had trained herself for that. It was part of her big project, to be as still as possible. She wanted to be unmoved.

I first met her at the gym. It was early in the afternoon and busier than I would have liked. People, on the whole, make me nervous, but not because I'm insecure. I'm self-employed and live alone. I prefer my own company and keep my own time. I've become very good at finding the quietest possible time to do anything, and I've been a regular at the gym for a while. Like any habitat, it has its own rhythm, a circadian flow. Once you know how it goes, it's easy to make it work for you.

At the crack of dawn, you get the suits. They'll do a quick run before a heavy round of weights. The routine is half performance, half ritual. They attend to each body part efficiently, with precision. They shower with expensive lotions before putting on their expensive shirts, fastening the buttons in the mirror like rich people on TV. They order cabs and make stops to buy coffee, extra hot. They go to work in big glass buildings and watch the doors to their offices open and close while they remain seated the whole time. In some ways, their goals are just like hers – optimise the movement so that later you can afford not to move at all. After that, there are the 'morning people', full of energy, smiling at everyone, failing to notice when no one smiles back. They're creepy and cheerful, like cheap actors in advertisements, ones for laundry detergent maybe, or pasta sauce in a jar. It depresses me, the way they act like each day is a gift instead of something that accidentally happened to them. Then, you get the parents and carers, fresh from the nursery drop-off or the traffic jam at the school gate. They'll come in with some child's accessory – kids' headphones, a miniature water bottle, a towel with cat ears. It's like they don't even notice the thing is too small, like they're just giant people holding regular-sized stuff. Then, there's everyone else: students, bartenders, night-shifters, drifters, chronic insomniacs, and people like me who keep their own time.

Between two and four – my preferred hours – the whole place feels light and calm. Between two and four, people keep themselves to themselves. They listen to their podcasts and watch TV on the little screens. They mind their own business and don't put too much of themselves into the world – their own vibes or ideas or whatever. They take their time, they don't injure themselves. It's during the pre- and post-work rushes that you see the sprained ankles and pulled knees, locked shoulders, muscle spasms. Early evening is the worst. People arrive anxious, with a desperate kind of energy. You can see the colour of it in the air, greyish-red and out of focus, like brake lights in the fog. That's when the most serious damage occurs. I've seen all kinds of things. A tangle on the leg press, a snagged zip and a bloody mess, a concussion from a bad snatch. Once, I saw a man break a leg just doing star jumps on the mats. And even when there are no injuries, there's a lot of unkindness around. People who are mean to themselves are often mean to others too. You can feel it when you get too near them, a shiver of warning that says to steer clear. I never used to pick up on that kind of stuff but, since I started taking care of myself, I've become more sensitive to all kinds of things. I've got this whole new way of knowing, just by feeling how my body responds. Muscle twitches, leg cramps, tight shoulders, shallow breathing. It's a language I've acquired, one of the many things she validated for me. When I met her, I wasn't in great shape. I couldn't run very far and I didn't feel good. Though I was naturally strong, I was tired and angry all the time. I was one of those people wasting my energy, getting cross with myself and being unkind. It's taken a lot of muscle work for me to get to my personality, to make the change there too.

When she arrived at the gym that first day, the receptionist tried to direct her to the changing rooms but she ignored them and walked right in. She was wearing a shell-pink shirt, grey chinos and lace-up boots. A net bag hung from her wrist, with a water bottle, a watch, a notebook and pencil and some small plastic items – make-up or deodorant, vitamins perhaps. Among the grey and black machines, between the gleaming mirrors and the miniature televisions, surrounded by people in shiny leggings with go-faster stripes on their shoes, she looked like something from the past. She was a faded photograph of a 1940s factory worker, an early feminist icon. I got the impression that she didn't care what we thought. She wasn't there to play a part in someone else's spectacle because she had her own goals in mind. That's one thing she's taught me about focus. When you're walking your life path, doing your life's work, the other stuff will fall away. It's been a good lesson for me, and I feel lighter having learned it. Imagine a dog coming out of the sea after a long, cold swim. You've had a good time in the water and now you're shaking yourself free.

She looked around, and when she couldn't see what she was looking for she came to me. Her hips swayed as she walked. She moved slowly, holding my gaze.

'Are you Simon?' she said. Her voice was soft and low. She tipped her head to one side.

For a moment, I thought I would lie and say yes, but I stayed quiet.

'Or do you know where Simon is?' she said. 'Simon's doing my induction today.'

I told her I wasn't Simon but that I knew who Simon was. Everybody knew Simon, he was that good-looking – one of those people who might accidentally become famous at any moment. I put the dumbbells on the rack, walked a loop round the gym and returned to her.

'Simon's not here,' I said. My throat was dry and the words came out strange. I coughed and then apologised. All the while she looked at me. 'Try the desk,' I said, shifting my weight from leg to leg.

Her hair was shiny, there was a flush in her cheeks. She made me nervous, but it felt good. I liked being near her and that was something new. Most of the time, strange people made me nauseous. People in general gave me a headache. But she was a pleasant change, like a refreshing breeze. She smelled of mint and something sweet.

Reaching into her little net bag, she pulled out the watch. 'I'm early,' she said. 'I'll ask at the desk.'

Once again, I heard the receptionist point her in the direction of the changing rooms. Then, when Simon was finally located, he too asked if she wanted to change her clothes.

'I'm fine,' she said curtly. 'I'm quite happy as I am.'

He looked her up and down. 'All right,' he said. 'If you're sure.'

She dropped the watch back into the little bag.

Anticipating Simon's arrival, I'd moved to the lat pull-down, put it on the heaviest setting and was struggling to keep form. I tried to steady my breathing. I didn't want it to look like hard work. At any moment, I thought, Simon would touch her. A hand on her back to guide her, an encouraging shoulder pat. The idea of it gave me a queasy feeling – a tingle that ran through my arms and made the weights drop down with a crash. There was something special about her and I wanted to be the only one to see it, for her to be a mark of my excellent taste. She was like a rare painting, some subtle work of genius, a thing that no one knew to look at until the expert told them it was there. I still feel that way about her sometimes, even though I know a lot of other people are watching her too. I still feel that it's me who really sees her, the truth of her, all the way down.

Simon was saying something quietly about the lost property cupboard.

'I can move perfectly well in these,' she said. Her voice was steady and clear, much quieter than his. She tugged the fabric of her blouse. 'Stretchy,' she said.

'Okay,' said Simon. 'Each to their own.'

Simon was used to people fawning over him, trying to impress him or make him laugh. They would giggle and touch their faces and blink too much. He had symmetrical features, the perfect physique. His hair was thick and, when he stood beneath the air conditioning unit, it moved in graceful waves. He was jacked, but it didn't look like he'd had to work for it. Rather, it looked like the muscle came first, so why wouldn't he use it to lift weights?

'Let's see you do a stretch,' he said. He glanced over at me then, trying to catch my eye. He was smirking, handsomely. I turned away, pretending not to have seen. I didn't want to share in the joke, not at her expense, behind her back.

'What kind of stretch?' she asked. A few people were looking over. There was some giggling by the treadmills. She didn't appear to notice, and when I glared at them they turned away.

Simon launched himself into a runner's lunge. He placed his hands on his front knee and the tops of his arms bulged. He signalled for her to copy him, which she did with ease. Then he did a forward bend and some calf and hamstring stretches, and again she followed his lead. She was large, broad in the shoulders with big, strong hands. When she righted herself, her blouse had shifted and part of her bra was exposed, grey and opaque, like an industrial contraption. She didn't move the blouse to cover it. Instead, she focused on her movements, concentrating hard. I saw she was flexible, long-limbed, and that she held herself well. When Simon demonstrated a position, she could always execute it more fully than him. Her body made lovely shapes – balanced and rounded and elegant.

'Great,' said Simon, but he didn't really mean it. He was annoyed to have been wrong about her clothes. 'Cool,' he said, in the same false tone. 'Good start!'

'What now?' she asked. She didn't appear to have any

feelings about the fact that he had made her stand in the middle of the room doing pointless stretches, while other people slowed their running and rowing to look. When new customers sign up for the gym, they're supposed to feel wrong about themselves. Their leggings are too tight or too loose, their bra straps and shoelaces need constant adjustment. They check their phones every couple of minutes, willing the time to pass, hating themselves for being weak, slow, misshapen. But there she was, in the middle of the room, surrounded by strangers, lunging and bending, revealing her undergarments without a second thought. Not knowing things didn't make her anxious. Being new didn't make her anxious. She didn't care that her clothes were all wrong. All she wanted was to learn, and there was something childlike about that. It drew me to her because it was endearing, but also because it was a quality I would have liked to possess myself.

Simon couldn't get a read on her. It was strange for him to be around someone who so clearly didn't care what he thought. He had the kind of charm and good looks that made you desire his approval, even if you didn't like him that much. From time to time, he'd give me compliments – 'Great session, my man!', 'Hitting it hard over there!' – and, against my better instincts, I'd find myself grinning back at him, eager and pathetic. I was glad if he noticed me, and I often saw his personal clients competing for his attention. But whatever it was about Simon that made a mockery of the rest of us, she was immune to it.

'Hold this,' she said to him, handing over the net bag.

He took it gingerly, letting it hang from his fingers as though it might be unclean.

She rolled her shoulders, then made circles with her arms. She moved her head from side to side to stretch her neck and winced a little. 'I'm not warm enough yet,' she said.

Simon pointed to the mats where I was loosening a muscle I'd pulled on the too-heavy weights. 'Finish up over there,' he said.

She didn't look over and she didn't move. Instead, she said: 'Here's fine.'

In the middle of the room, she stretched her body in all directions while Simon stood at her side, smiling awkwardly and shifting the bag from one hand to the other. A few times, he looked in my direction, but I didn't engage. It was fun to see him like this, not knowing what to do. When she finished stretching, she shook out her whole body, starting with her feet and moving upwards. Her hips made broad circles. She swayed her head like something possessed. She let the shaking pass through her in a single, continuous wave. It looked inhuman. A controlled electric current, or an earthquake slowed down. It seemed too private an act to witness, a deeply intimate thing. Half the room had paused what they were doing to watch. She untied her hair and let it scatter, then, with a black elastic band, she twisted it into a ball on top of her head.

When she turned back to face Simon, he flinched.

'Now we can start,' she said.

He showed her the treadmills and the cross trainers and the recumbent bikes. The afternoon light was beginning to change.

It flooded the windows yellow and deep and made fist-like shapes on the floor. The gym was filling up now. Music rattled, feet pounded. I was tired. I hated the sound of it when it was busy like that – too many people heavy-breathing, a collective rasp in the air. Ordinarily, I would have gone home, admired the sunset on my way back. Instead, I followed them round the room, trying to keep an appropriate distance, putting the machines on their lowest settings so I could concentrate on her. I wanted to hear what she had to say. She'd given me that cool and pleasant feeling – so rare for me. I was hopeful that, if I stuck around, I would feel it some more.

I couldn't hear much until there was a pause between songs, a long gap while someone changed the radio station or searched for a playlist on their phone. 'When you're doing cardio,' Simon was saying, 'you need to keep your heart rate up. You shouldn't take long breaks between machines. It's not good for your metabolic rate.'

She nodded, her limbs moving mechanically on the cross trainer.

'You need to keep up momentum,' he added, 'if you're trying to shed the pounds.'

I looked up at that.

Abruptly, she stepped off the machine. 'Sorry, what?' she said. The plastic feet of the cross trainer kept on moving without her. A new track came on, something light and tinny. Their voices rose up through it.

'It's not helpful if you're looking to, you know, slim down a bit.'

Her eyes narrowed and her mouth became small. The blood rushed into her face. She had stopped too quickly. She took a deep breath and turned to face him, standing with her feet wide apart.

'Looking to slim down,' she repeated.

'You know, if that's your goal.'

To be fair to Simon, he was a product of his environment. It wasn't entirely his fault that he lived in a world that made a lot of money by encouraging people, especially women, to hate the way they look. It was early January then, and all the posters in the foyer were for the gym's *New Year! New You!* campaign. Every day, people were signing up for his personal training programme which promised *transformation* and *a new lease of life*. In the foyer by the toilets, there was a germ-caked noticeboard where members could post their *before* and *after* photographs. The *befores* were always blurry and dull. Nobody was allowed to smile in their *befores*; the whole idea was to look heartsick and oppressed. The *after* pictures, by contrast, were crisp and bright. They were edited with strange, unnaturally vibrant filters, and taken at flattering angles, to sharpen the cheekbones or narrow the nose. In the *afters*, you had to smile like one of those animals whose face just accidentally makes that shape, an axolotl or a quokka.

It should have been clear to Simon that she was never going to be interested in the *before and after* experience. If he had been paying attention to her as I had been, he would have known that hers was a particular mission, that she had more imaginative goals. But he was used to his regular clients, to their nervous smiles and their deference to his biceps and expertise. I suspected that he had never had to think very carefully about his words before. Perhaps she had presented him with a whole new experience – the suggestion that he might change his behaviour to accommodate someone else.

The music stopped then came back on, some kind of moody techno track.

'I'm not here to lose weight,' she said.

'Right,' said Simon. 'Of course not. No one's suggesting—'

'You were suggesting.'

Simon said nothing.

'I don't hate myself,' she said.

'Of course.'

'I don't want you to find me attractive.' She was speaking very slowly, as though addressing a small child. 'I'm here because I want to be strong.'

Simon laughed nervously and took a step back.

'Is that something you can help me with?' she said. She was almost shouting now, the way my mother used to talk to my grandmother, though my grandmother's hearing was always fine.

Simon nodded.

For a brief moment, she looked exhausted. Her shoulders sloped forward and her eyes seemed to shrink. It's interesting to recall that, back then, her face was still so expressive. At some point, it became much less flexible, a smooth and empty surface, a glass pebble or a china dish.

'Lifting weights would be a good way to get strong,'

she said. 'If I lift some weights, I'll get bigger rather than smaller, won't I?' The music filled the room with new intensity, gloomy strings and heavy bass. She turned to face him square-on. Several people had removed their headphones or turned down the sound on their TVs. A few slowed their pace in order to give their full attention to the real-life drama playing out by the recumbent bikes.

I had never seen Simon look embarrassed before. His forehead was red and there were angry blotches on his cheeks and neck. He folded his arms behind his back and wriggled his fingers around the insides of his elbows, then made an effort to recover himself.

'We can do that, sure,' he said.

'What do you know about strength training?' she asked.

'I can show you,' he said.

'What can you show me?' she said.

He put a hand on her arm to take her over to the weights and the benches, but she recoiled.

'Sorry,' he said. 'I'm sorry.' As he led her across the room, he looked unusually small.

Quietly, without drawing attention to myself, I went with them, sliding onto a thicker mat to do some half-hearted sit-ups.

'Are you training for an event?' he asked. 'Do you have particular goals in mind?'

'I'm not sure you'd understand,' she said. Then, more kindly, she added: 'I'm not sure I can explain it to you.'

'Are you looking to improve your mental health?' he asked,

but quickly saw that this too could give cause for offence. 'I don't mean that you need to, just that – exercise can be – it can be hard – having mental health, or not.'

'Yes,' she said. 'You could say that's what it's for.'

He looked relieved.

'Is that why you do it?' she asked.

In that instant, I thought he might cry. He seemed vulnerable before her. 'I'm happier when I'm stronger,' he said. 'I don't get the weird dreams.'

She told him that she liked to meditate, and that if she were stronger, she would have more focus. She would be able to sit for longer and support her body more effectively. It was hard to be in the present, she said, but if her body were heavier and more in control then her thoughts would clear and her mind would recover its power. I wondered, between sit-ups, what it would mean to have a powerful mind. A powerful mind without a purpose seemed like quite a dangerous thing. I thought how satisfying it is when you plug in your phone after the battery dies, the moment you see the bright light come back on.

'That's great,' Simon said, almost his normal self again. 'I've just started meditating myself. With an app.'

She nodded her approval.

'Have you, like, studied it and stuff?'

'I'm working on my own technique,' she said, edging closer to the weights, running a hand over the dark metal surfaces. Neither of them seemed to have noticed my being there. I had this wonderful quiet feeling, moving backward and forward, up and down – sometimes in time with the music, sometimes falling behind the beat – and all the time watching her to see what she might reveal next. People who find exercise boring simply haven't learned to appreciate the soothing effects of repetition. Once you're absorbed in a rhythm, the world becomes larger, more interesting, and your sense of self becomes small.

They started with the kettlebells. Simon demonstrated the manoeuvres first. He bent forward at a perfect right angle and grabbed a weight with both hands, then he straightened his body and swung upwards in a slow and glorious arc, moving smoothly, like a machine. Muscles bulged above his knees and tiny veins poked through his arms. All the while, his face remained blank. After a few repetitions, a film of sweat came up on his brow but his expression did not change. Her previous hostility appeared to lift. She walked a circle around him as if he were part of an exhibition, taking care to appreciate, from all angles, the way the light hit. Simon was graceful. He made it look easy. I liked to watch him, too. There's something hopeful about a person who can make something difficult look effortless. More things become possible.

He showed her the various moves you can do with a kettlebell – swings, squats, presses, snatches – and she paid close attention. Then, at last, it was her turn. She was already pretty strong, but she didn't have his style.

'You're not breathing,' he said to her. 'You'll find it easier if you move with your breath.' He stood next to her, breathing loudly, making cartoon gestures for inhale and exhale. The movements came more naturally. Her jaw relaxed, the lines in her forehead smoothed. He'd show her the proper form for a particular kind of lift and she'd repeat it as best she could. He'd make some small corrections and she'd do it again, more accurately. From time to time, she took notes and drew diagrams in a small lined book. Sometimes she made him hold his position for much longer than was comfortable, so when she'd finished his knees were trembling and he was out of breath.

Towards the end of their session, they did one-armed pendulum swings together. Their breathing synchronised and they made good shapes. They moved more slowly than the music, which made the music seem wrong and not the other way around. The sun was low in the sky by then. As they raised their arms, the weights glinted, throwing back chunks of orange light, while their shadows were long against the walls. When I looked over at the tall windows, there were birds silhouetted against the clouds. The geometry of the city stretched out below. It felt as if something important was happening, energies converging, outside and in. I lay back on the mats and did a few reclined twists. I was content. I stretched my neck to one side and then the other as they completed their last triumphant revolutions with the weights. I'd stayed an hour longer than planned and my body ached, though my mind was alert. Simon guided her through a warm-down but she didn't like the stretches he suggested. She had her own versions, she said. I allowed myself a lingering look at her face, which seemed wide open and serene. Then I made a mental note of the time and the day, in case that would become her regular slot.

'So if you have any questions, feel free to ask,' Simon said. He was edging slowly towards the door. He lurched to open it from too far away, then stumbled and pulled it too hard. The hinges groaned. 'After you,' he said.

'I'm not done,' she replied.

'No?' he said, deflated. He was pale, a little grey. She had worn him out.

At this point, Simon would usually have begun his sales pitch, talking through the various plans and schemes, offering a personal discount which was, in fact, the advertised price. He opened his mouth a little. He made a quiet, rasping noise.

'Good for you,' he said finally. 'Stay as long as you want.' I heard him tell the guy on reception that he was going to take his break.

She went over to the rack of hand weights, opened the notebook and placed it on the floor. Before picking up the weights, she rehearsed the manoeuvres, repeating them over and over, eyes closed.

I stayed for a little longer, though I was tired too. I lay back on the mats, only now and again remembering to stretch. I couldn't stop thinking of her. I thought of her while I showered and dressed, while I walked the short distance to my home.

Things have changed a lot since that first day. She's kind of famous. Or at least, she has a lot of followers online. People admire her authenticity, her focus and determination. They say the way she holds her body is a kind of truth. It's easy to look back now and feel that her life was destined to unfold this way – I've forgotten the tiny moments where she might yet have taken a different path. But there was something about her, even then, something powerful and hard to describe. I still remember how it felt to be near her, because I felt it deep beneath my skin.

Two

She did not come back the following Wednesday, or any other afternoon that week. I know this for certain because I went every day and waited for her. I thought about asking someone at reception if they'd seen her, but I caught myself in time. I knew how it could look: a strange, quiet man like me asking questions about the woman who liked to lift weights in her low-cut blouse.

After a couple of weeks, I found myself in phenomenal shape. The sheer number of hours I was putting in at the gym was saving me money on utility bills, which was easily countered by the amount of food I was having to eat. Four or five meals a day barely took the edge off my appetite. I was falling behind on my work, building crazy amounts of muscle and never showering at home. My mother sent me an email because I was never free to answer her calls. *Dear Elliot,* she wrote. *Have you been abducted by aliens? Or, less likely still, have you met a girl?* I felt terrible then. I love my mother very much; we speak on the phone every day. She likes to know how I spend my time so that she can tell me where I'm going wrong. I emailed back saying things were busy, which felt shallow and insufficient, but it turned out to be true in a prophetic sense. A couple of weeks later, I took on a big job and there was no time for the gym anymore.

I have a system for times like these, when there's a huge contract to fulfil and limited time to do it. It's necessary if you're freelance, when there are months of nothing and then months of hell. It works like this: I do a big shop online, from a pre-saved list – tinned beans, microwaveable rice, avocados, oven chips, bourbon biscuits, dates, hazelnuts, spicy ketchup, frozen vegetables, soup cartons, pineapple juice, stimulant tablets, full-sugar cola, almond butter, cream crackers, and a selection of canned fruits. I start the day at six and do an hour of work before breakfast. I get in another five hours before lunch. I work five and a half hours between lunch and dinner, and after dinner I'll do a further three or four. If I'm lucky, I get five hours of sleep a night. To sleep any longer would make me stressed, which in turn would make it harder to sleep. I prepare three simple meals a day, all strategically timed. Breakfast takes fifteen minutes; lunch double that. For dinner, I allow three quarters of an hour, including preparation and washing-up. A couple of years ago, after another big job, I bought a top-of-the-line speaker shaped like a hand grenade. If there's time to spare before dinner, I blast out some music, which I think annoys the neighbours, but feels necessary. Sometimes it takes a lot of noise to clear your mind, to make your body relax again. And I don't really care about the neighbours. I have to listen to their screaming brats all the time.

I watch an hour of television before bed, but nothing goes in. It dulls the anxiety of the task at hand and sometimes helps me to problem-solve. If you can stop thinking consciously for a while, then your mind gets to work by itself. There have been times when I've been sitting, vegetating, and suddenly, out of nowhere, a solution arrives. I'll make a note and go back to the television. Then, the next morning, I have a head start. When I first began getting big jobs like these, I didn't have any of these strategies in place. I ate while working and hardly slept. My desk chair was too small for my frame and, if I was sitting in it for a very long time, it was as if my body would try to contort itself and shrink to fit the shape. After a couple of days, I'd be in all kinds of pain. It wasn't productive. I couldn't do any work and I got very sad. You have to find ways of managing yourself – physically and mentally. You have to have structures in place to make sure you get out of your own way.

In the early stages of hibernation, I thrive. I like my own company and the monotony of an overwhelming single task. It can be relaxing. It's like being on holiday – you're stuck there for a period of time, so you may as well try and make the best of it. But after a while something changes and the work weighs down on me. Often, I don't register the shift until I see the difference in my face. Lines appear across my forehead; my skin turns slightly grey. The whites of my eyes become soupy with bits of yellow floating around. A total lack of social interaction makes your features go kind of blank, as if the person behind them isn't really there. In spite of the fact that I'm a loner – *a hermit,* my mother says; *a creep,* according to my sister – even I cannot survive the world alone. I don't need friends or a girlfriend, perhaps, but I do need stimulation. I need people to smile at, frown at, to roll my eyes about or whatever, because while I'm working my face goes numb. The muscles relax when there's no one around to bother arranging them for, and then they stay there, downturned and miserable, until I drag myself back into the world. Over the years, I've had to find ways to cope. Talking to myself in the mirror, doing karaoke at my desk. Language-learning podcasts are useful because they force you to repeat things and to move your mouth in unusual ways. Italian is good for its stressed and elongated sounds (*buon pomeriggio!*) and Mandarin for the musicality of the tones (*wǒ xiǎng yào mápó dòufu*). Hungarian has far more sophisticated consonants than English (*a számlát, kérem*), while Thai has forty-four consonants and thirty-two vowels. I was always good at languages at school, but I had no use for them. Now they help to keep my face in working order.

When a big job comes to an end, any feeling of satisfaction is quickly overshadowed by intense anxiety. After a prolonged withdrawal, it can be hard to re-engage with the world. I get scared. I have to really will myself to do it. It takes great strength of mind. I think about the brightness of the sun, the cool breeze on my skin, the thick metallic smell of the weight machines. I make myself nostalgic over the texture of newspaper pages, or the sweet dogs I see tied up by the corner shop. I gather courage by shouting at my own reflection when I turn the computer screen off. Mostly, I use stuff my dad used to say to me – *What kind of man even are you! Carry on like this and you'll be dead before you've ever been alive!* – and then I drag myself to the gym, thinking of all the nice things I might do afterwards, like watching movies with Kirsten Dunst in them, or buying some coke from one of the students who live downstairs.

The job I took after I met her was one of the biggest I've ever done. My whole life was on hiatus. I didn't leave the house for a month. While I was working, I stopped thinking about her, but as soon as it was over she came right back. All those mental images I'd taken, they were the first things to return. This time, I wasn't so nervous about leaving the house, because all I wanted was to see her again. There was a sense of purpose to my going to the gym, like I was on some kind of quest.

I packed my bag, slung it over my shoulder and walked out the door. I was ready. She was going to be there, I felt sure of it. It was as if I could make it happen just by wanting it so badly, and when I thought about really seeing her again my stomach did a spin. I scanned my card, burst into the changing rooms and put on my kit. As I passed reception, I waved to Simon and held the door open for a skinny brunette. I looked around. The room was busy. Bright morning light cut the floor into squares. I squinted. She wasn't on the treadmills or the bikes. She wasn't using the weight machines or the monkey bars or the exercise balls. The battle ropes were all occupied by short men with overbuilt shoulders. But there was plenty of time. I had a whole regime to get through, and because I was out of practice it was bound to be slower and more painful than usual.

'Not seen you for a bit,' Simon said, creeping up behind me without making a sound. He was wearing those running shoes that aren't really shoes, just rubber feet.

'Had a lot of work on,' I said, knowing what would follow.

'Yeah, but mate,' he began, 'that's when you need it the most. You put work in, you get more work out.'

I nodded, shamefully. 'Finding time, isn't it,' I said.

He shook his head slowly.

'We've got some new toys,' he said. 'I'll introduce you.'

Simon stayed with me for the whole session, pushing me harder than I wanted to go. The new kit was a heap of weights that looked like sandbags. I pictured farm labourers from god knows when shifting sacks of grain onto carts. I was born three hundred years too late, I thought. I shouldn't have to go to such lengths, to pay a monthly membership fee, to spend so much time in this sad, grey room. My movements ought to contribute to some kind of common good. But, for me, in this modern world, I would call my mother at the end of the day, she would ask what I had done and I would have to tell her that I picked some things up and then put them back down in the same place.

Simon was having girlfriend trouble, so while I sweated my guts out, he talked non-stop.

'She can't be quiet,' he was saying. 'Like she has to make a noise the whole time, like she's scared of there being no noise.'

I tried to murmur something to say I understood, but it was too much, holding my core, concentrating on the weights, all while keeping an eye on the door in case she arrived.

'Sometimes,' Simon continued, 'you just want to sit. Reading the paper, or texting, and you just want to do that quietly. But she goes on and on. She can be putting on lipstick, texting her mate and talking to me all at once.'

After an hour and a half, I told him I was done.

'No way,' he said. 'A round on the kettles and you're good.'

I tried to protest, but he was already hanging the weight in my hands.

'She even talks in her sleep,' he said.

I groaned by way of response.

'What would you do, if you were me?' he said.

I rested the weight on the floor and wiped some sweat from the backs of my knees. I scanned the room again, making sure she hadn't slipped through the doors while I was bending down. I had been so sure that she would be there, had convinced myself just by willing it so.

'Do you remember that girl?' I said. 'The girl who did her induction with you?'

'Which girl?'

'Old-fashioned shirt,' I said. 'Shiny hair.'

Simon thought about it, then shrugged.

'I asked you a question,' he said. 'What would you do?'

'I don't know,' I said to him.

He waited.

'Honestly, I like being on my own too much to ever get to that point.'

'You're a smart guy,' he said. 'I should try that myself.'

'You've never been on your own?'

'Never seems to fall out that way.' He counted me through the last few reps, then cleaned the weights with a damp cloth.

'Have you seen that girl though?' I asked again. 'The one in the pale pink shirt.'

'Enough on my mind with the girl I've got,' he said blankly.

After I'd showered and changed, I surveyed the gym once more. There was still no sign of her. Simon was finishing his shift and asked if I wanted to go for a beer. I said no, because I was starting to feel anxious about being out of the flat for so long. You can't do too much at once after a period of confinement. You have to break yourself in gently, reintroduce yourself to the world in easy steps.

'Smart man,' he said again. 'Knows what's good for him.' He said it as if there was someone nearby who might appreciate this information about me, but there was no one.

For the next few weeks, each time I pushed open the swing doors to the gym, I had a little nervous feeling in my stomach. Each time, I thought, it became more likely that she would be there. A lot of the muscle had returned to my arms; my thighs were bulking out. I did sessions with Simon and he talked about his girlfriend, all while stacking up heavier and heavier things for me to lift. I don't think he was doing it deliberately, but as a training strategy it wasn't bad. He was never quiet for long enough to give me a chance to complain. My strength returned quickly. I started to look like I had before. I told myself that when she did come back to the gym, I'd be ready for her.

Three

One morning, I made a stop at a café and ordered two fried egg sandwiches. I hadn't eaten eggs in years. The sandwiches were awful. The ketchup was cheap – too thin, acidic – and the bread was like memory foam. It crept up around my teeth and, for the rest of the day, I found myself pulling bits of it out of my gums. The coffee arrived with an oily film, contaminated by the fat in the air, while the eggs themselves were slimy, but with a decent fried taste – blackened at the edges, which was how my mother used to make them for me. There were only three people in the café – me and two old guys reading newspapers, both facing away from the counter, lifting their heads to look out the front window from time to time. One of them kept peering at me around the side of his paper. He had sunspots on his cheeks. His skin was beige-grey, as though it had been washed with the wrong colours. When I put my money on the table and got up to leave, both men said goodbye to me. I found this touching. It was almost unbearable. *I love you*, I wanted to reply, but didn't. Instead, I nodded and tried to smile in a meaningful way.

Walking to the gym, I felt queasy, worse than if I hadn't eaten anything. I paced up and down the car park. I took deep breaths and my stomach growled. When I got to reception, there was a new kid on the desk.

'Hello!' he said brightly. 'Can I help you?'

I shook my head and my stomach made an obtrusive sound. The kid coughed, as if to cover it up.

'Have a great session!' he said. 'Don't hesitate to ask if there's anything you need!'

In the changing rooms, I caught my reflection and was disappointed to see how tired I looked. I'd been sleeping fine since the big job finished, but the older I got the longer my recovery time seemed to be. I'd rest for eight, nine, ten hours a night, and still I was exhausted, like all the tiredness I'd ever felt was racking up behind me.

'This is why you're here,' I told my reflection, out loud. 'To stop yourself turning into a sack of shit.' I splashed some water on my face.

I dug around in the bottom of my gym bag for headphones. I found a motivational playlist. With the music too loud, I had a go on a treadmill. After fifteen minutes of angry running, I felt better. The music gave me a headache but I didn't want to turn it off. It was one of those days where everything took more energy than I was willing to give it, where I felt the full weight of my body and the effort it took to keep dragging it around. I was considering what to do next – the sandbag weights or the arm bicycle – when I felt something, a little shiver, a new pulse in the air. I pulled the headphones from my ears and looked around. There was a faint rush of dizziness as I stepped off the machine. I steadied myself, gripping the arm of an unoccupied cross trainer, and then I saw her. There she was.

She was facing the mirrors, doing squats with dumb-bells in her hands. Because of the angle of the reflection, I could see all of her at once. It was thrilling to get the full scope of her, all three hundred and sixty degrees. I tried not to look too strangely, too intensely, in case someone noticed and told me to stop. I went over to the weight machines and sat on the leg press. From there, I could get a good view without drawing attention to myself. She looked amazing, kind of huge, a lot of muscle but fat as well. Sweat dripped from her hairline and pooled down her back. There were large wet patches under her arms and on the backs of her legs. On her feet she wore a pair of proper weightlifting pumps, the vintage ones like bowling shoes, with cream and navy stripes. Her little notebook was propped against the wall. I squinted to see the open page. It showed a strange, geometric shape – a letter, or a symbol perhaps, but not one that was part of any language I knew.

I had to remind myself to keep my legs moving on the machine. I tried to synchronise movement with breath so that it would become a natural reflex and I could give her my full attention, but I was still tired and, since coming off the treadmill, the uneasy feeling in my gut had returned. I put the headphones back on to cut the hum of the machines and the tinny radio playing through the speakers. I flicked through songs on my phone and found something with strings and spiritual noise. The eggs settled at last. I felt calmer, more alert.

It was good to look at her. Everything about her suggested power and strength. Her form was perfect. The angles were precise, rounded neatly at the corners by the muscle she'd built. Her hair was looped in a knot at the top of her head. Plant-like tendrils drifted down around her face. She did everything slowly, taking long deep breaths, working through the difficult transitions with grace and ease. A new song started playing. There was a shift in the light. It came in mellow and warm. In the mirrors, her face glowed, like a romantic painting in an old museum. She put down the dumb-bells and moved to the mats. She did one-armed push-ups and burpees, but slowly – as if she'd changed the speed settings of her body, as if she might also fast-forward or rewind. My view of her was partially obscured by the lat pull-down and the red-faced man making use of it. I went over to the abduction machine. When I looked up again, she was holding a side plank. Her top leg was lifted, making pretty circles in the air. I checked the clock above the door and timed her. She stayed in position for almost nine minutes, then did the same on the other side. All the while, she appeared relaxed. She wasn't forcing herself to do anything, it seemed, because whatever she did was exactly what was required.

After a series of body weight exercises, she did some stretches and I noted that she'd maintained her flexibility in spite of the muscle she'd gained. She made graceful lines with her arms. Her eyes were wet and glistening. I reached for my phone. I held it down by my leg, like I was just checking something, reading a message, skipping a track. I opened the camera, lined up the shot, flicked to video, zoomed in. The light changed to her advantage. The long shadow of her body rose up the wall. My hand slipped. I took an eight-second-long recording of my knee. After that, I lost my nerve.

When she'd finished her stretching, she sat cross-legged on a yoga mat with the notebook laid out in front of her. She took a pencil from her bag and began to make rough marks across the page. I couldn't see clearly but it didn't look like she was writing anything. She was drawing, not a figure but another strange shape. I leaned forwards, trying to get a better look. I put one foot on the floor for balance and leaned further. I was still looking over, completely absorbed in her, when she put down the notebook and got to her feet. She started walking towards me. She was looking right at me, no mistake. I straightened myself and tried to move my legs. I had a horrible cramp down my left side. I willed myself to move, but could not. As she closed in on me, my hands were sweating, my throat was dry. I expected her to say something but her lips were drawn firmly together. The cramp intensified. My arms began to shake. She waited a moment and then she gave an exaggerated curtsy, deep and low, like a concert ballerina. Her mouth curled up at one corner in a malicious smile, and then slowly, purposefully, she walked out of the room.

A few people stared, but I shrugged it off. I went through the rest of my workout – weights, then stretches – without having to exert the same effort as before. I didn't think she was angry with me. Rather, I sensed she was amused. Flattered, even. Maybe she'd wanted me to look. It was the beginning of something between us, I thought. A point of connection, a shared moment. It was progress.

When I got home, there was admin to do. The big job had gone well and there were emails thanking me, offering more work. The money was considerable. If I'd said yes, I could have sent my mother on some enormous holiday, or given myself a few months off. But I didn't, because I wanted to see her. I wanted to be part of her world. For the first time in my adult life, I wanted new routines.

Four

For a while, I really pushed myself. I built stamina and worked on my form. I was sleeping well and taking supplements. I drank three litres of water a day. I made smoothies with juice and spinach and chalky powders in pastel colours. She had exercised some influence over me. The thought of her – how she moved and walked and changed the space around her – had, in turn, begun to change the way I wanted to live.

I liked to imagine her in other environments, trekking through forests or swimming in fast rivers. I pictured her on the beach – stretching, making her strange drawings – against a backdrop of vast water, with grey skies and jagged driftwood, gusts of wind picking up the sand. I wondered what her *real life* was like, if she had a job or parents or friends. It was hard to see her in normal situations, sitting at a desk, catching a bus, making sandwiches, watching TV. I wanted to know what she was eating and if she put special products on her skin. I wanted to know if she had any pets, or if wild animals were drawn to her. We saw each other regularly at the gym. We'd exchange nods as we came in or out, mumble *hello* by the water tap. I wasn't yet brave enough to start a conversation, though I'd rehearsed a variety of plausible scenarios in my mind. It went on for a long time – me watching her, her looking up every now and again and nodding my way. But eventually, we did speak.

It was a Saturday. There was a large group of teenagers in the middle of the room. They were hanging off one another and squealing, pushing each other around, grabbing at one another's caps, bags, pockets. Usually, I hate it when people in the gym stand around wasting time like that, but with teenagers I don't mind so much. I feel sorry for them: almost grown with nowhere to go, all that energy and nothing to do with it but dangerous driving. Under normal circumstances, I wouldn't have been there on a Saturday, but the kids upstairs had their recorder lesson and were playing 'Greensleeves' at half speed on a loop. I was practising round-the-world pull-ups, which Simon could do easily and I could not, when I heard a strange noise. It sounded like something feral, a stray animal come in from outside. I listened harder and the noise came again. Other people could hear it too. A brief stillness came over the room. Then, I saw her on the mats.

She was hinged at the hip. Her legs were straight and her back angled forwards. Sticky-looking bits of hair fell down over her forehead. There were heavy dumb-bells in her hands.

One leg trembled lightly and all the veins were raised in her arms. I wasn't sure what to do. I didn't want to alarm her by running over, but it seemed unkind to just stand there and watch. Perhaps it was a serious injury. I couldn't leave her, wailing like that. No one else seemed to know what to do, so I went over, moving softly, like you would if you were approaching a wildcat.

'I'm stuck,' she said. 'I can't get back up.' A squeaky, growling sound came from somewhere deep inside her. A thread of sweat trickled down her nose and onto the floor.

'It's all right,' I said. 'I'm here.' I felt confident. Powerful.

She growled again, impatiently.

I took the weights from her hands, resting them on the ground. 'Does it hurt?' I asked.

Her eyes rolled. 'Lower back,' she said, panting. Her face was red, turning purplish. Huge tears swelled in her eyes.

'Is it in spasm? Can you feel something moving?'

She gave a louder, high-pitched yelp. The whites of her eyes were bloodshot. Her neck looked sinewy and tense. 'Get help,' she said through gritted teeth.

A crowd of people had formed around us. Some were pretending to be concerned while others gawped open-mouthed. Simon wasn't there, nor were any of the personal trainers. Through the glass doors I could see the new guy on reception, playing with his phone. I stood up and turned to the crowd. 'Someone get help,' I said authoritatively. 'Ask for Simon, or Marina, or Jan.' I liked the sound of my voice right then. It was deeper, more masculine than usual, which felt right for a crisis. My better instincts had kicked in, I thought. I knelt down again beside her and touched her head very gently. I was doing really well.

She started shaking, violent jerks from head to toe. She put a hand to her chest. She was struggling to breathe.

'You're having a panic attack,' I said.

'No shit,' she replied, spilling some drool from the corner of her mouth.

'Try to focus on your breathing,' I said. 'Breathe in and breathe out.' I tried to breathe with her. I made big, breathy movements with my hands.

To my surprise, she did as I told her, and her cheeks paled. The muscles in her neck relaxed, and her arms hung loose.

Just then, Simon appeared – tall and handsome and glorious. The crowd made way for him.

'What have we got here then?' he said, bending down so that his face was next to hers. I remember thinking that his voice was much softer and lower than mine. It had a lilt, as though he were about to tell us a story, some kind of parable from which we would emerge as better versions of ourselves. For a few moments, I just watched him. I didn't listen to what he was saying or how she responded. I admired the shape of his body, his elegant shoulders, the strong line of his neck. It was sickening, but compelling. He made me feel terrible about myself. It seemed intimate, what was happening between them. He was whispering to her. His lips were close to her ear while she cried big, silent tears. I stood up and moved away. The afternoon light, though grey, became bright and intense. It brought the room into sharper focus. I had the sense that something important was taking place, that something miraculous was about to occur. There would be a transformation, a religious conversion, and all of us would leave the place changed.

Simon kept on whispering while a pop song jangled from the speakers – a boy singing dolefully, rhyming 'space' with the other kind of space. The onlookers began to drift back to their machines. I stood there watching, transfixed and slightly weak at the knees. Then, out of nowhere, she straightened herself. She did it quickly and apparently without pain. The movement seemed to have shocked her, as though her body had done it of its own accord. Her eyes were wide and glassy and her mouth hung open. She stood there, looking at her hands, like a character in a movie who has come back from the dead.

Simon put an arm around her. 'Are you all right?' he asked in earnest. He too seemed shocked, surprised at the strength of his own powers. I wanted to know what he had said to her, which words were responsible for her recovery.

'Are you all right?' he asked again.

She nodded, then she burst into tears, collapsing onto his shoulder.

There was nothing for me to do but leave them alone. I'd been lurking there for long enough. Simon had outdone me in every way. I thought about resuming my workout, but it didn't feel right. I'd lost focus. I was drained. My senses must have been heightened because I was suddenly aware of the smell of the gym – old and new sweat mixed together, damp metal, damp towels. There were the dusty particles of floral deodorants and the complex rubber odours of communal yoga mats. The light seemed harsher too, artificial and glaring. The clouds had thickened outside. On the way to the changing rooms, my body felt heavy and accidental, like some outrageous accessory that I never should have bought. I was nauseous. The ground wobbled; the sounds around me were muffled and indistinct.

In the shower, the queasy feeling reached a peak. I caught sight of a wet hairball clogging the drain and thought I really might throw up. I tried thinking about other things, running lists in my head. I named all the symbols on the keyboard function keys, then I thought of all the emojis that have hands. I listed types of cloud, and then I tried to remember the many bus stops I used to pass between my childhood home and school. By the time I got to my final list – the names of my mother's nine aunts – the nausea had subsided a little. I dried myself and got dressed, but couldn't face the smell of antiperspirant. When I bent down to tie my shoelaces my head swam, so I lifted my foot onto the bench and tied them loosely, without looking down.

Before going home, I went to the cafeteria for a diet cola and a packet of crisps. It was what my mother used to give me when I got seasick as a kid. We had taken the Dover to Calais ferry once a year to get to Disneyland, where a long-time boyfriend of hers was a safety inspector for the spinning swings. As I sipped the cola and let a crisp dissolve on my tongue, my body temperature returned to normal. I thought about Disneyland some more. I hated that boyfriend; I'd always wished for his rides to break down. Even if I was on the ride as I was wishing it, even if the breakdown led to my death, I didn't care. If I died on his swings, she'd have no choice but to see him for the creep he was. The old hatred had a restorative effect. It was energetic, galvanising. As a child, I had fantasies of newspaper headlines. *Swing Massacre. Disney Child Killer.* I imagined a trial, no appeal. Parents outraged, worldwide; my mother being interviewed on the news. I wouldn't have died, no, but I might have been hospitalised. Eventually, I would have made a miraculous recovery. A thousand times a day, I'd hear my mother repeat: *I nearly lost everything, what a lucky escape.* I smiled at the memory as I finished the crisps and my stomach felt good. Briefly, I entertained the idea of putting my gym clothes back on and finishing up my usual routine, but just then, as I was tipping the last of the cola into my glass, she walked in and she waved at me.

Her face was broad and glistening, her hair was matted to the top of her head. She ran a hand over her forehead to keep the sweat from her eyes. A few people in the café turned to look. She had put on a sheer white blouse, her green sports bra showing clearly underneath. Her leggings had bunched at her thighs and there was a hole in the knee I hadn't noticed before. She was barefoot, leaving a trail of footprint sweat marks on the greying tiles, carrying the weightlifting pumps in her net bag. Her expression was bright, happy and open, and what my mother might call *wholesome* or *fresh.* There was colour in her cheeks and her eyes were clear. I thought that perhaps she was going to walk right past me, that she had in fact been waving at someone else, but then she stopped at my table and put a hand on the chair across from me.

'Can I sit here?' she said.

'There?' I asked.

'Here,' she said, pointing very clearly at the chair.

I mumbled that she could.

She sat down. Some sweat from her ponytail dripped to the floor.

My first thought was that she must be angry with me for abandoning her while injured, or for not providing her with the right kind of help. It seemed reasonable. I had not been enough for her – she'd had to wait for Simon to come. I was angry, too. I was filled with loathing and regret. I thought of the fairground swings again, chains snapping, screams in the air.

I waited for her to speak first, but she didn't say anything. She sat there quietly, looking at the empty cola can on the table.

'Are you feeling all right?' I asked.

'Much better,' she said, pleasantly. 'It was nice of you to help.'

'It looked serious,' I said.

'It wasn't serious.'

Silence resumed.

'Do you want another cola?' she asked.

I told her no thanks.

'I'm hungry,' she declared. 'Are you?'

I shook my head. 'Crisps,' I said.

'You want some crisps?'

'No, I just had some.' I looked about the table for the empty packet as proof, but it was no longer there.

She ordered at the till and came back with a pint of water, a slice of cucumber floating in it, then sinking. A few minutes later, her food arrived: two portions of beans on toast, a large bowl of wilted spinach, a chocolate brownie, a flapjack, an apple. She set to work.

I felt like I ought to be talking to her, entertaining her while she ate, but I had nothing to say. She had this bizarre effect: it felt so good to be around her, but at the same time it filled me with dread. I wanted to give her things, to do things for her, though I couldn't think of anything she might need from me. I looked through the large windows and down at the car park. I thought about checking my phone but didn't. The radio was on and the presenter was giving the weather report.

'More rain,' I said, but the words came out so quietly that she couldn't hear me over the sound of her own chewing.

When she had finished her meal, she sighed. 'When did you start lifting weights?' she said.

'About a year ago. When I quit my office job.'

She smiled. She almost looked normal. 'I quit my job too,' she said.

'How's that working out?'

'Perfect,' she said. 'I don't ever want to work again.'

I laughed. 'Sounds good to me.'

'I mean it,' she said.

'Good for you.' It came out more sarcastically than I'd hoped. I felt my face redden. I could see right through her shirt. There was sweat dripping down her neck and over her collarbone, making it shine. There was sweat on her wrists, a pale gleam.

'You have beautiful form,' she said.

'Sorry?'

'When you're lifting, you have beautiful form.'

'Oh.'

'How did you learn?'

'I guess from Simon, and the others.'

She shook her head. 'That is not how you learned.'

'What do you mean?'

'They're interested in strength and aesthetics. You're interested in something else, the way the movement makes you feel on the inside.'

'Am I?'

'Yes,' she said. 'You know you are.'

A warm feeling gathered in my chest. She was right, in a way. I didn't go to the gym just because it made my arms bigger. I went because it stilled my mind. Somehow, she had understood this and I felt good about her knowing it, like maybe I'd been doing the right thing all along.

'I have a book,' I said.

'What book?'

'A book of photographs.'

'Oh?'

It wasn't a book that taught you how to exercise or lift weights. I wasn't into self-help. It was a proper photography book, with moody pictures in black and white. I'd found it in a charity shop one winter, while shopping for Christmas presents. I thought about giving it to my mother, who sometimes pretended to be interested in art, but in the end I kept it for myself. It seemed to me that the photographer's subject was not the weightlifters' muscles, but their ability to concentrate. The people in the photographs had a sense of purpose. They believed in themselves. I hadn't known that photography could convey something like that, that there could be pictures of all these different people and somehow, in the end, in this shared pursuit, they could all look the same. I tried to describe it to her. She looked at me intently while I fumbled my words. I was boring her, I thought. She didn't really want to know any of this. I stopped talking. She kept looking at me.

'Can I see it?' she asked.

'The book?'

'Can I see it?'

'It's at my house.'

'Okay,' she said slowly. 'Can I see it at your house?'

'You don't know me,' I said.

'No.'

'I could be someone really weird.'

'It's okay if you don't want me to come to your house,' she said.

'Yes, you can come,' I said. I felt a small panic rise in my chest. It wasn't often I had guests.

She stacked the empty plates and pushed them into the centre of the table. When she rose from her chair there was sweat all over it. It took a long time for her to put on her shoes. I got up and found myself standing awkwardly by her side. Other people were looking at us. I didn't know if I was proud or ashamed and, feeling conflicted, I stared at the floor. I kept my head down as we crossed the cafeteria, and again as Simon called goodbye.

Outside, cold air rushed into our faces. The street was crowded and we walked in single file. I felt I was watching myself in a movie. The light was brighter than usual, the sounds of the world more distinct. Music playing from someone's car seemed to capture the moment and my feelings about it – anticipation, desire, a heart beating, heavy dread.

'Can I shower at your place?' she asked when we had reached a quieter part of the road. She jostled her shoulder against mine. I held my breath. I nodded.

As we got nearer, anxiety took hold. I couldn't remember what state the flat was in. What if I'd left something embarrassing somewhere or forgotten to pick up my laundry? What if last night's washing-up was still in the sink, or the patch of damp had returned to the ceiling? Most alarming of all, what if she saw something awful that I just hadn't noticed? Some detail, some object, some arrangement of things in a space that would expose me as freakish, intolerable, disgusting? As I catalogued the flaws in the plasterwork and all the chores

I ought to have done, I gave myself a headache. In the lift, I started trembling. To my surprise, she reached out, put a hand on my arm and squeezed it tight.

'You don't need to be nervous,' she said.

I looked at her.

She gave my arm another squeeze.

I tried to read her expression as I opened the door to the flat. Perhaps she felt sorry for me. As she took in her surroundings, I watched her. Did she think it was too small? Too dirty or too clean? Did it smell strange to her, even when it smelled normal to me? Did the furniture seem too large, or the paintwork too dull? I noticed a small brown mark on the skirting board that I had never noticed before. I thought how large my shoe rack was when I only had three pairs of shoes. But her expression didn't change. She said nothing, not even a thank you as I ushered her into the kitchen or when I put a glass of water in her hand.

She asked to be shown to the bathroom and didn't make any comment about it having no windows and no bath, just the shower cubicle in the corner and a tiny beige sink. I gave her my best and largest towel.

'There's the shampoo,' I said.

She shrugged. 'I don't use it.'

'You don't use shampoo?'

'I make my own, mostly lemon juice.'

'I could get you some lemons,' I said.

'It isn't Thursday,' she replied.

While she showered, I rushed from room to room,

rearranging the coasters on the coffee table, the mugs in the glass-fronted cabinet. She emerged, wrapped up in my faded purple towel. When I asked if she needed fresh clothes, she said no. I put the photography book on the kitchen table. She sat down and ran her finger over the cover, eyes wide.

'I can leave while you change,' I suggested.

'Not yet,' she said. 'I'm not quite dry.'

I sat down next to her and she opened the book, examining the subjects carefully. She leaned in close to the images, sometimes tracing a muscle-curve with a finger, sometimes lifting an arm to recreate an angle or rolling her shoulders in sympathy.

'I'd like to be in a book like this,' she said.

'You want someone to take pictures while you work out?' I asked, remembering my own failed attempt to video her.

'I'd enjoy it, waiting for the picture to be taken. Being still for a really long time.'

I didn't tell her that I thought the photographer was capturing motion more than stillness, that the weightlifters really had been lifting weights. She seemed to like the idea that the compositions were staged because this would, in fact, require more effort and more strength. I thought about how it would feel to lift a weight only part way up, and hold it there, unfulfilled. It wasn't possible. It would be unbearable.

'I could look at these all day,' she said.

'You can borrow it if you like,' I said, and immediately worried that I'd made it sound as if I wanted her to leave.

'No need,' she said. There was a pause while she adjusted

the towel, then ran a hand through her hair. 'But maybe I could come and see it again sometime.'

'Whenever you like,' I told her.

She flicked through the pages. She took photos of photos on her phone. When she had finished, her arm brushed mine. I looked at her, trying to work out if she had done it on purpose. She smiled at me, a vague little half-smile, then she leaned in again. I worried she was mocking me. She understood my desire and how it made me pathetic. Still, her body pushed against mine. The warmth of her skin, the relief of her spine – it made me feel safe in the way that children like to feel safe. It made me feel that she was something I could trust.

Five

She started coming over whenever we saw each other at the gym. At first, we just looked at the photographs. Sometimes she made notes. I'd offer her smoothies with supplements, crushed-up caffeine tablets and glutamine. They looked like ready-mix concrete, but she seemed to like them anyway. She'd drain her glass slowly, without coming up for air, then pour the dregs from the blender directly into her mouth. She helped herself to cereal bars and sweets and packets of crisps. I was always at the shop, stocking up in case she came round.

She was interested in the fact that I had adopted a plant-based diet.

'It's good to eat plants,' she said once. 'To take your nutrients from the earth.'

'It's good for the environment,' I said, though that wasn't why I didn't eat meat. I mostly did it because I was sick of people saying that you couldn't build muscle that way, sick of guys at the gym telling me about their high-protein diets, all raw eggs and steamed chicken and steak. My favourite foods are things that happen to be vegan without trying – curly fries, baked beans, spaghetti hoops, mushy peas, nut brittle, prawn cocktail crisps. One grey afternoon, I was making a smoothie for her with coconut oil, instant coffee, banana and Huel. The blender was loud, but she shouted over it.

'Have you ever wanted to be a plant?' she said.

'What?'

'Have you ever thought about what it's like—'

I turned the blender off.

'—to be a tree?' she yelled.

By that time, we were quite familiar with one another. I was comfortable with her long silences, the probing way she looked at me. I'd learned to expect these kinds of questions – conjured up from god knows where. *What's your favourite kind of moon? Do you keep a record of your dreams?* I evaded them where I could, or invented answers I thought she would like. I liked all the moons, equally. I told my mother about my dreams. In reality, I never told anyone that most of the dreams I had involved complex administrative processes: insurance claims and tax returns.

'No,' I answered, reluctantly, but then I realised this wasn't true. I had thought about it as a child. An uncle had asked me what I wanted to be when I grew up and I had pointed out the window towards a tall holly tree that belonged to some neighbours over the road. They'd all laughed. The uncle, not a real uncle but my mother's boyfriend's friend, joked that it would be better than going down the mines.

'Maybe when I was a kid,' I told her.

'Children are like that,' she said. 'They instinctively know what's good for them.'

'What about you?'

'All the time,' she said.

This, too, was characteristic. She'd lead you into discovering these strange things about herself, and then she'd just leave them there, hanging, as if you'd know how to respond. I tried to think of something to say but when nothing came to me, I turned the blender back on.

She was steadily building muscle. Sometimes, when she was standing in the kitchen doorway waiting for me to hand her some crisps or a grey-green juice, it would surprise me how much space she took up. Her shoulders almost touched the frame on either side. She was tall as well, almost as tall as me, and entirely unapologetic about it. She didn't stoop or let her shoulders curve inwards like other tall girls I had known. As she became stronger, her movements slowed down. She walked slowly, talked slowly. Even her breathing seemed slow. If she made a gesture with her hands, it always took a long time for the arc to complete.

One night, she came for dinner after a long session at the gym. I was cooking soya burgers and sweet potato fries. I'd put the fries on a tray when she came out of the bathroom wrapped in a towel that was much too small.

'You look amazing,' I said to her. 'Like something from the book.'

She was vast and smooth and gleaming, like an ancient statue, polished and still.

She came and stood beside me. I could smell my shower gel on her skin. It was green-scented and cooling. She was wearing my deodorant, maybe the aftershave as well.

'I could take your picture,' I offered.

'All right,' she said. She positioned herself against the pale yellow wall with her legs in a wide stance.

The overhead light was too strong. I turned it off and we were pitched into darkness. I found the switch for the cooker hood lamp. It cast softer shadows. It made the muscle of her legs stand out. I took three pictures. Each time I pressed the button, she was looking somewhere else. Once, straight to camera; once, off to the left, and finally, over my shoulder, gazing into the middle distance. Included in the frame was the handle of the steel fridge door, the corrugated surface of a radiator, dimples in the wall where the paint fell away. It didn't look like my kitchen anymore. It looked as if she was standing somewhere in the future, in another reality, on another planet. There were soft colours, sharp edges, uncanny patches of dark and light. I showed her the images and she was pleased. She sent them to her phone and spent a while zooming in and out, examining her shoulders, her wrists, the shape of her hair, the light in her eyes.

I poured her a glass of water. She took a long drink.

'Do these take a long time?' She pointed at the tray of fries.

'About half an hour.'

She loosened the towel and dropped it to the floor.

'The oven's not at temperature,' I told her, looking at the ceiling.

She bent over and slid the tray inside the still-cool oven, then she led me to the bedroom, took off my clothes and told me to lie down. We kissed a little, not a lot, and I slid my hands down the plane of her back.

'Slower,' she said.

I slowed down.

'Slower than that.'

I tried to think of myself in slow-motion video, the moment playing at half speed. I pictured her in the gym – the heavy, gradual movements that made it seem as though time passed differently for her.

Her body intrigued me. It was superhuman, overdeveloped, muscular and dense. Her skin was smooth and strong, as though it was thicker than normal skin. Her hair, too, was shinier and tougher than regular hair. She knelt beside me and ran her fingers over her face, drawing lines down her neck, over her breasts and torso. Her nails left white marks on her skin. Then she climbed on top of me and sank her hips down.

We lay there, like that. I didn't move. Neither did she.

'Is everything okay?' I asked.

'Do you want to stop?'

'No.'

'Well.'

'You're not moving,' I said.

'I like it this way.' There was a pause and then she said: 'This way, you feel everything.'

At first, I didn't know what she meant. I began to worry that I wouldn't feel anything, that it would be difficult to keep going.

'Relax,' she said, in a very low voice.

'I am relaxed.' I clenched my jaw.

'You're not,' she said. 'Keep still.'

I didn't move.

'Try breathing out for longer.'

'There's nothing left to breathe out,' I said. I didn't want to breathe on demand.

'Relax your face,' she said. 'If your face is relaxed, your body is too.'

Anger pulsed through me. Why should I relax? What was wrong with my face? I thought about pushing her off, about grabbing her arm in some painful way. But then she put a firm hand on my chest and breathed loudly, amazingly slowly, as if one breath might last five minutes.

I didn't do anything else, none of the things I would usually have done – the touching of hair or the kissing of shoulders. I just lay there, very still, with my arms and legs like dead weights on the mattress while she shifted her body in tiny increments up and down. It was disempowering, I suppose. Maybe that's what she wanted, what she liked. After a while, it started to work, and it was good.

'Close your eyes,' she said.

So I did.

Light glowed red through my eyelids. My skin came alive. At one moment, the pleasure seemed to be coming through the soles of my feet; at another it was rooted deep down in my ear. Bright lights shifted strangely in the dark. Sensation accrued slowly, swimming through me in ebbs and flows. At a certain point, I knew she was trembling and I had a feeling like déjà vu, thinking we had met before, that this was not the first time. But it wasn't that exactly. Somehow she'd unsettled a memory of sexual freedom, of something curious, unthinking and open. It reminded me of being very young, when I still didn't know very much about sex and it seemed like something good and clean – long before it became complex and shameful, the kind of thing people's parents had opinions about. When it was over, we lay next to each other, perfectly still and in silence.

We each ate two burgers and a plateful of chips. We drank pineapple squash and then warm oat milk with amaretto syrup from a squeezy tube. I offered her sweets but she refused so I ate them all myself. She told me she would stay over, and I said yes, though it hadn't been a question. When she fell asleep, I spent a long time watching her. I took more pictures of her on my phone, from different angles, at different heights. It was like a game of Russian roulette: would she wake up or would she not? Looking back on it, though, I bet she knew what I was doing. I bet she pretended the whole time.

Six

We were only really together for a few weeks. Probably *together* is too strong a word. She liked me well enough, but already she was focused on her goal. Each time I saw her, she was bigger and stronger than before; more solid and more at ease. There were moments of intimacy – a sudden confession, a sad smile – but they didn't last long. They were often followed by distant periods when she became silent and withdrawn. Other people might have found this rude, but I knew her better than that. I didn't make any demands of her. Maybe that's why she kept me around so long.

After we slept together, it didn't seem like there was anything weird about my watching her while she worked out. She knew I was doing it, and now and then she'd glance over in my direction and offer a half-smile. Her lifting technique was flawless, each movement symmetrical and in perfect alignment. It was like watching an intricate mechanism, a well-made hinge on a beautiful door. We didn't talk much in the gym, but it was an amicable not-talking. We each had our own work to do. We respected one another that way. It's a powerful thing to acknowledge another person's ritual behaviours. It's a special kind of understanding that takes place.

One evening, in bed, I asked her if she would spend my birthday with me. I'd been thinking about it for some time. I don't usually celebrate birthdays; they drift by like any other day. The only difference is that, when my mother calls as usual, I have to listen to the story of my birth – the pain, the near-fatal blood loss, the emergency doctors, the tunnel of light. I say *thank you* and she says *you're welcome*, but she always sounds evasive, as though she hasn't yet decided if it was worth it after all. And that's it, the only concession to an otherwise ordinary twenty-four hours.

But this year was different, thanks to her. She agreed to come over. Then she smiled at me and touched her hair, like she was just some ordinary girl. I still hadn't mentioned her to my mother, not because I was trying to be secretive but because I didn't have much to say. She had never invited me to her home. I didn't know where her money came from. She'd quit her job, she said, but I had no idea what kind of job it had been. Did she live on her own? Were her parents alive? Could she drive? Who paid for the gym? I realised the only scenes I could picture her in were wild landscapes – haunted woods and lunar deserts. Places that were dreamlike and unreachable. Places other people were not. When I thought of this, I felt angry. Why did she share so little of herself with me? I was always telling her things. There was the Disneyland boyfriend, my mother's obsession with filtered water, my sunscreen phobia, the recurring dream I had about finding myself dead in a plastic bag. I told her these things, in part because I knew she wouldn't judge, but also because, sometimes, one of us had to speak.

On my birthday, I ordered dinner from a vegan junk food place. There were lumps of crispy stuff that looked a bit like fried chicken, an oddly pale mac and cheese. I lit candles, found a new playlist, and put on my best camel-coloured shirt. Just when I felt that everything was ready, she sent me a text saying something had come up, she wouldn't make it after all. I didn't know what to do. My body tensed all over. I got a horrible ache in my jaw. The food would go to waste. I felt stupid, all dressed up in my smart clothes. I had a cry, drank a beer, sat down in front of the TV. I was hungry, but didn't want to eat. Two hours later she sent another message saying: *Change of plan. On way.* I washed my face. I felt stupid again, for feeling stupid before.

She arrived around half past nine, hugging three bottles of wine. We'd never talked about it, but I'd assumed she didn't drink. It's something people have wrongly assumed about me too, because I don't eat meat, but I've never been interested in clean eating or detoxification. I just don't like the idea of all that dead stuff.

'I didn't know what you'd like,' she said, presenting me with the bottles. 'And I'm thirsty.' She laughed nervously, sounding a little out of control. She seemed smaller. Her shoulders were hunched. One of her hands was trembling gently. 'Nice shirt,' she said. She kissed me twice on the neck. I wondered if she'd been drinking already.

I asked if I could take her coat but she seemed not to hear me and instead bundled it onto a dining chair. Her hair was wet from the spring rain. One after another, she went through the kitchen cupboards until she found a pair of wine glasses that had once belonged to my grandmother. She rifled through a drawer for a corkscrew, opened the white and poured herself a large measure, which she drank in one long gulp.

'Are you all right?' I asked.

'Great,' she said flatly. 'I feel so energised today.'

'You went to the gym?'

She shook her head.

'Meditation?'

She shrugged.

I poured my own wine – it didn't seem she was going to offer – while she helped herself to a swig of orange juice from the fridge.

She sat down at the table and tapped her nails on the surface. The heels of her shoes clicked against the kitchen tiles. I realised that was why she looked so different. She was no longer still. Her whole body was moving: a tremble that seemed to start in the gut and spread outward.

I busied myself laying the table. The food was still sitting in a large paper bag on the countertop, untouched. I took out one box then another to reheat in the microwave. She stood up and sat down several times. She came over just to touch me – a stroke on the wrist, a hand on my back and then in my hair, small kisses on my ears. When I tipped crackers into a bowl, she put an arm around my waist. When I topped up her wine glass, she licked my neck. I liked the attention, but it made me nervous. I had never really understood her, but whatever I had come to expect from her was now, inexplicably, incorrect. With the second glass of wine, she settled a little. Her fingers kept up their rhythm, but her legs and feet stilled. Briefly, I recovered some optimism for the evening ahead. I kissed her forehead and refilled my own glass.

She raised her glass without looking at me. 'Happy birthday,' she said to the table, then picked up a cracker and let it crumble between finger and thumb.

'What's going on with you today?' I said, more assertively than I'd meant. I tried a spoonful of mac and cheese from the box and found it tasted intensely of coconut.

She stared at the wall. She put the wine to her mouth but didn't drink. Her teeth rattled on the glass.

'You seem nervous.'

'Coming from you,' she said, meanly.

I didn't ask her anything else.

We were silent while I transferred the food onto dishes, spooning out heaps of not-sausages and not-cheese pasta.

'Cheers,' I said, raising my glass to her.

She said nothing but speared an enormous lump of not-chicken with her fork before opening her mouth very wide to get it all in. It was rude, but it was also kind of hot. At least her appetite hadn't changed. She ate vast platefuls. I suppose it soaked up some of the wine.

When dinner was over, my stomach ached but her mood had softened again. While I cleared plates and bowls into the sink, she picked up a bottle of red. Without asking, she turned off the music. She filled both of our glasses this time. She asked if I'd bought dessert but didn't wait for me to answer. She'd been thinking about her ex-boyfriend, she told me. She wanted to forget all about him, but couldn't. He kept finding ways to creep back in. I had never heard her mention any previous relationships. I had never heard her talk about anyone else at all. She explained that she was only just beginning to make sense of what had happened to her, how these experiences had prepared her for the next phase of her life.

Seven

There were no long silences, none of her usual awkward questions. Instead, she produced a steady monologue, running circles, tripping over herself. I had to concentrate hard to keep up. The things she said were not easy to hear and, once I knew the whole story, part of me wished she had kept it to herself. It made her seem ordinary and complicated, where before she'd been magical, unreal – something better and more pure than everyday life.

She began by saying she was sorry she had never invited me round to her house. I told her not to worry, and that I was always happy to have her at mine. This was a lie: she made me anxious. I still worried about what she might uncover. She explained that she'd never been able to invite me over because she had no place of her own. She was living with a friend, having moved there after the break-up and then staying much longer than she'd planned. I didn't really want to hear about her exes. I didn't want to think of her with anyone else. I wasn't even sure I wanted to know about her friend.

'You're okay with me telling you this?' she asked.

I forced my body into a relaxed position. 'Tell me anything,' I said. I prepared a list of all the things I could think about if it got too much. Fruits that are really vegetables, popcorn flavours, the stages of grief.

The ex-boyfriend's name was Paul. She'd met him at work – a law firm. They'd started their jobs around the same time. I told her she didn't seem the lawyer type, that I was starting to wonder who she was at all. She laughed, and put a hand on my shoulder as though to say, *and why would you know anything about that?* Then she drank some more wine and carried on. In the beginning, Paul had been sweet and shy. He'd needed a lot of reassurance, he'd wanted her to be with him all the time. When he made a decision, she would have to tell him, over and over, that he'd done the right thing, only later realising that she didn't know what the right thing was. I couldn't imagine her with someone like that. She tended so thoroughly to her own needs; when would she have had the time? It occurred to me that the person I knew her to be hadn't existed very long. A few months earlier, she had been living an entirely different life. She was a stranger to herself.

'That sounds tiring,' I said dutifully. I gave her my best listening face.

She shrugged. 'I didn't mind it at the time.'

After a year or so at the firm, Paul had started to gain

confidence. He became more independent and made his own friends. She had found it interesting to watch him change. His voice had deepened, it seemed to get louder, which meant that other people paid more attention to him. With this positive reinforcement, he began to stand taller, to put his elbows on the table during meetings, to interrupt. There had been a sweet spot, she explained, a year into their relationship, when she had stopped worrying about him – he didn't need her reassurances anymore, he hardly asked for her opinion on anything. For a time, they were happy. She introduced him to her mother. They moved into a beautiful house. But his evolution did not stop there. Paul became arrogant, self-interested, small-minded. He had stopped seeing her as her own person; instead, she became an extension of him. Whenever she did anything or said anything, he understood it as a reflection of himself. He found it impossible to understand that she might want to do things for her own sake.

As she told me this, her posture changed again. Her body curved in on itself. The line of her mouth shrank and turned down. For a moment, I thought she might cry. I wasn't sure what to do if she did – that wasn't part of our arrangement. I realised how simple our relationship had been up until that point. She had only needed me to watch. I was her first viewer, her first subscriber, her first *like*.

Briefly, I left the room, to see if she might recover herself. I brought chilled water from the fridge. When I returned, her face had reddened. It didn't seem like grief or betrayal or anger, but humiliation. She was ashamed. She downed the water in two long gulps and wiped the drips with her cuff.

'He never hit me,' she said carefully. 'And it wasn't always that bad.' She placed her hands together, carefully, in her lap.

'He didn't hit you,' I repeated, bracing myself. 'Did he do something else?'

She told me that Paul had become increasingly paranoid. He always wanted to know where she was. If she went for lunch with a colleague, there would be questions at the end of the day. What had she talked about? How far from the office had they walked? Did she even like Mexican or Japanese or Turkish food? Who paid? How could he know she was telling the truth? He undermined her at work. He'd joke: was she pulling her weight? Was she up to scratch? During this time, she said, she had attended a weekly painting class. This was the one part of her story that made sense to me. It was easy to imagine her with paintbrush in hand, the sole authority over her canvas. But Paul resented this too. He told her she was embarrassing herself, that she wasn't a creative person, that it was humiliating to pretend otherwise. When she was invited to social events, he'd make sure that she couldn't go. At first, she said, he did this *nicely*. He would plan for them to do something else, something special that he knew she would like and therefore would not refuse. But quickly he ran out of ideas and had to come up with a new strategy. He found ways of making her stay late at work, manipulating their boss and colleagues into thinking she might not be doing her share. But this was a risk, he might raise suspicions among their co-workers, so again he was forced to change tack. Eventually – she said this quietly, not looking at me – he started asking her to spend long periods of time in a particular room of their house. Sometimes she went willingly and sometimes he locked her up.

The room itself was small, on the top floor. The internet didn't reach it. It wasn't large enough for a bed. They called it *the box room*, but she said it was more like a large cupboard. There was a sloped ceiling, precarious shelving, a small window with a broken latch. There was just enough space for a narrow desk and a few old suitcases piled on the floor. The first time he put her in there, she'd been on her way out to meet her mother for dinner. It had been arranged for weeks. Paul told her to cancel and she would not. He said she was selfish, refusing to see things from his point of view. She'd wanted to see her mother, she explained, because it had been a long time. Her mother was an unhappy person, and always alone. She had been doing her hair in the mirror that hung on the box room door when he came towards her, standing too close. He wasn't taller than her, she said, but he was stronger than her back then. He pushed her into the room, shut the door and told her to make the call. He gave her excuses: she'd stayed too late at work, she wasn't feeling well. When she told him she couldn't lie, he said she lied all the time. When she threatened to call the police, he opened the door, took the phone from her hand and locked her in. He texted her mum with some odd but plausible excuse and never let her see the reply. Then he left her there until morning, when she went to work without having showered or slept.

She looked at me carefully. I tried to keep my face blank.

'Do you understand it?' she said.

'What?'

'Why he did it.'

'Of course not,' I said. Who could understand a psychopath like that?

She shrugged. 'He's not a monster,' she said. 'I think, to him, it felt like he had no choice.'

After that first time, he started locking her up more often. While she learned to recognise the warning signs, she never knew how to calm him down. Several times, she repeated that he was *not violent*, by which she meant he did not punch or push or kick her. He didn't rip out her hair or destroy her things. He didn't take her money. He was not sexually aggressive. She'd read a lot about domestic abuse and it didn't seem to her that her case was that bad. She wasn't sure what would have happened if she had struggled against him when he led her to the room, but she never did and so now she'd never know. Rather than arguing with him, or trying to free herself, she developed coping strategies. If you give it enough time, she told me, you can get used to anything.

One of the suitcases in the box room contained a folder of important documents, which held their degree transcripts, bank records, identity papers, insurance policies. Sometimes, when she was bored, she'd take his counterpart driving licence or his birth certificate. She'd tear off a minuscule part of the paper, slowly eating away at the evidence of his life. She hid a blanket in another suitcase, and a flat old cushion to serve as a pillow. Behind some old books, she kept moisturiser, a toothbrush and toothpaste, along with her notebooks, some pencils, a sketch pad.

I wanted to ask her why she hadn't told anyone what was happening, or why she didn't think to run away. I tried to put myself in her position. I would never have put up with it, I thought. I could never live like that. But then, for a moment, in the fibre of my muscles, I got a sense of it – the exhaustion, the wearing down that made it impossible to reimagine your life. I remembered the Disneyland boyfriend, how he hated my sister and me. How he could be threatening towards my mother, and the things he said to her when he thought we were asleep. How we always went to see him, no matter what, and how relieved my mother would be on the ferry home.

Eventually, something did change. She was sleep-deprived and hungry after living in the box room for nearly a week. She'd been barred from the rest of the house, allowed only to wash and dress before work. Sometimes Paul gave her dinner and sometimes he did not. She never had breakfast. She read the same book four times. If he was feeling lonely or struggling with a difficult case, he would sit outside on the landing and tell her what was wrong. She would counsel him through the door and then, if she felt she'd been helpful to him, she might try and ask for something – to use the shower, or to make a cup of coffee. Often, she said, in a conciliatory tone, on nights like that he would say *yes*. On other nights, he sat downstairs with the television blaring, while she was left alone. If she needed the toilet, she had to bang hard on the door. He would shout: *Are you being serious? Are you just messing me around?* When she cried and said that she was serious, that she really did want to go, he would escort her down the hall to the bathroom and watch her while she peed. She was malnourished, bone-weary, on the edge. What she had hoped would be an odd phase, another stage in his psychological growth, became their way of life.

My phone rang – my mother, the birthday call.

'I should take this,' I said, but she appeared not to hear me. 'Is it all right if I take this?' I tried again.

She looked at me vaguely then carried on with her story. A minute later, I saw my mother had left me a voicemail. I knew she would be angry. We always talked on my birthday. I tried not to think about it. I ate a handful of crackers, though I was already much too full.

One day in autumn, a friend at work – Susie – had found her trembling in the break room. When Susie asked if she was all right, she had wanted to say yes, but her body shook violently and gave her away. She started to cry. When she tried to recover herself, the trembling returned more forcefully than before. Susie cancelled her meetings. After seeing a doctor, she was signed off work for three weeks. Susie offered her spare room. That was how her transformation had begun – in a city-centre apartment, where someone had taken care of her for the first time in her adult life.

She lifted her palms to her face, then sighed.

'What now then?' I said, meaning: what would we do with the rest of my birthday?

'I'm going to be completely self-sufficient,' she said.

I pictured a static caravan, a generator, eco-plumbing.

'I'm going to live alone and only do what feels right.'

'Good for you,' I said, though I had no idea what she meant.

She went to the kitchen and came back with a bottle of sparkling wine. She pulled the cork then dropped it, letting it roll about on the floor. She filled our glasses and the bubbles rose up. I put my lips to the glass and felt the froth against my teeth.

'Did I wish you happy birthday?' she said.

I sipped the wine. It was too fizzy, like a sponge. My body felt warm and heavy. I had lost my ability to concentrate. I wasn't used to listening to other people for so long. I wanted her to need me, but not like this. I liked her strength, her independence. I liked the person who only needed me to watch and to say yes. My head ached. I was sad for her, but I was sad for myself, too.

Without thinking, I turned on the television. We watched the news, then a panel show. She dozed a little, her head resting on my shoulder. I kissed her gently and let her drool on my shirt. After we had sex, I felt pretty good about myself. I thought I'd done something worthwhile. It was generous, I thought, that I had listened to that whole story about cruel Paul and sweet little Susie. She slept heavily while I lay awake.

My heart was beating too fast, as it always does when I've had too much to drink. I was too hot.

In my mind, the boyfriend was small and mousy, a miserable example of a man, while Susie was like the best friend from a 1990s romcom – skinny, clear skin and a chic little bob. Probably Susie wore a lot of pencil skirts and cute but sensible shoes. Probably she was really organised but sometimes forgetful in an adorable way. Probably she had a little dog. Everyone knew a Susie, I thought. The boyfriend was more difficult. I couldn't see why he'd go to such lengths. What was in it for him? He could have chosen a simpler, more solitary life, surrounded by things that were much easier for him to control. It had been a very strange birthday, I thought. And then I remembered that my mother had called. In her voicemail, she sounded excitable. *I hope you're doing something fun, Elliot!* she said. *It is your birthday, after all!* Then, more soberly, she added: *Everything is always so serious with you.* When my mother said that she loved me very much, I felt a weight on my chest. I looked at her, the strange woman sleeping beside me, and wondered what the hell I was doing.

In the morning, she was quiet. I guessed she had a headache too, so I put some painkillers on the kitchen table, along with a carton of juice.

'How are you feeling?' I asked.

She was standing in the doorway, stretching her hamstrings, lifting one leg then the other, reaching forward to touch the toe.

'Can I borrow some shorts?' she asked.

'What for?'

'I'm going to the gym.'

I found some shorts, burgundy with a white trim. They looked good on her. I offered her a T-shirt, which she refused in favour of the roll-neck top she'd been wearing the night before, but she took some football socks and wore them pulled high up her legs. She tied her hair back with an elastic band and then she ate five slices of toast. She kissed me goodbye – not a real kiss, the kind that just lands in the air. She squeezed her large hand around my arm and thanked me for dinner.

I unlocked the door and watched her walk down the hallway to the lift. Then I watched her as she pushed the button and waited. I watched as she adjusted the socks, pulling them closer to her knees, and fiddled with the elastic band in her hair. She must have known I was standing there, looking at her, but she did not turn. Later that day, I drafted several text messages.

Thanks for last night.

I'm here for you.

Don't forget to bring back my socks.

I never sent any of them. It wasn't necessary, I told myself. She would soon be back. She had confided her secrets in me. I was sure we would be together, in a real relationship, from that point onwards. I was buoyant, optimistic, contemplating my future with her, as though I had passed some kind of test.

Eight

That was the last time I saw her in real life. She didn't text and she didn't call. She quit the gym – Simon told me, when I asked him, shamefaced. She stepped right out of my life. It hit me pretty hard. Only once she'd gone did I understand how much of my energy she'd taken up. Without knowing it, she had become a guiding principle, a light towards which I tried to grow. I tried to remember what life had been like before her. It hadn't seemed so awful then.

I took on another big job. It was a dark time for me. Initially, I stuck to the routine. I worked out in the evenings, ate regular meals and slept five hours at night. But I couldn't keep it up. The work was too much. I stopped exercising, so I had no appetite. I didn't eat or listen to music or learn any languages. I didn't do a big shop or leave the house for tea and bread. I sat at my desk, occasionally forcing myself to dip a stale biscuit into black instant coffee, and did my best to apply myself to the task at hand.

The job was time-consuming but not difficult. I was busy but still I was bored. My mind remained free to replay everything she had ever said to me. I tried to rationalise and explain. She was traumatised, I thought. She wasn't thinking straight. But eventually, as with all things over-intellectualised, I understood there was no real problem to solve. It was all very simple: she had other things to do. She was moving on.

Therapists will tell you to find a narrative, to put a story around your sadness. But when something happens that makes perfect sense, that you understand completely, that's when you've got nowhere to go. There's no therapeutic jour-ney, no moment of epiphany, just a slow and depressing climb towards acceptance. That's much harder than learning to tell stories about the people who hurt you in the past. It means acknowledging that, for them, you were insignificant, a stop along the way.

When the job ended and I emerged from my sad hiber-nation, I found myself in a sorry state. My skin was a mess, covered in spots and scarred in the places where I'd scratched and picked them. I was chronically dehydrated, having drunk mostly coffee for a month. The mere idea of going outside for more than ten minutes filled me with dread. My palms became hot and sweaty, and the wasted muscle tensed in my arms as if I were preparing for some kind of attack. I tried testing my voice in the mirror. 'Come on,' I said. 'Buck up.'

It was raspy and weak. I had no projection, no tenor note. I tried ironing my clothes, cleaning my shoes, cutting my nails. I practised conversations in the glass door of the microwave.

'Good to see you again!'

'How have you been?'

I put on a range of different facial expressions – sad, glad, calm, normal. They were all disturbing, somehow unreal.

I had to start small. First, I went to the shop to buy fruits and vegetables, beans and rice. There was a new person on the till, which saved me the bother of saying too much. We merely nodded at one another. I made lunch. I downloaded an app to remind me to drink ten glasses of water a day. I did eighty press-ups in the morning and eighty sit-ups at night. Everything ached: not just muscles but other, more internal things – bones and the insides of bones, and then whatever's inside that. I slept heavily and that was what healed me in the end: hours upon hours of sleep.

The first time I went back to the gym, the receptionist seemed shocked by my appearance.

'Have you been in hospital?' he asked.

'What? No,' I said.

'Never mind,' he said, looking confused.

Simon asked me if I'd had the norovirus, because apparently a lot of people had. 'My sister got it,' he said. 'And my god, did she look like hell.'

'Thanks a lot,' I told him.

I tried my usual routine on the weights and found I could hardly lift a thing. My arms had shrivelled; all the tone in my shoulders was gone. I was ashamed and weak, but at least I had something to focus on. I wanted my body back. I wanted to be strong. Just like her, I wanted to recover a sense of control.

At first, I set goals. This many kilos, this many reps, but the pressure was counterproductive. I remembered what she'd said to me – that my movements came from inside – so I tried to take each day as it came and to only do what felt good. Once I stopped expecting things of myself, I achieved much more. I no longer obsessed over the limits of my body: instead, its limits held valuable insights, the very keys to success. In a few months, I learned how to do round-the-world pull-ups just like Simon. I deadlifted heavier than ever before. Sometimes, other people at the gym would ask me for advice as though I worked there, as though I looked like the right person to trust. I smiled at them generously. I pointed to Simon. *That's your guy*, I'd say, then wait to see if they looked disappointed. I still thought about her a lot. I longed for her to see the good work I had done. I still expected that, one day, she would come back.

Nine

It was Simon who showed me her videos. At first, I didn't believe him, but when I looked closely at his phone I saw that it really was her. She was standing in some kind of garden, surrounded by trees and plants. Her proportions were gargantuan, she had finally metamorphosed completely. Her muscles were rounded and glistening. She appeared elegant, ultra-modern, ethereal, like something dropped down from outer space. With Simon and the guy from reception, I watched one video after another, mesmerised. She was meditating, but not in a way I'd ever seen before. She adopted strange positions and inhabited new shapes. Still, the feeling she evoked in me was familiar: calm and satisfying, like remembering a word for something you've been trying to describe for a long time.

I was glad to see her, even on screen. I didn't know quite how to act. The videos felt intimate. Watching them made me feel close to her again, as though she was sharing some precious part of herself. But at the same time, she was no longer mine. Simon and the receptionist and anyone else who cared to look – they too had access to her.

Later that day, I sent her a text. *So you make videos now, you OK?* She didn't reply. A fresh wave of anger surfaced. Did she think I'd just forget about her? I'd played my part in her transformation, after all. She owed me a note of acknowledgement, at least. For a few hours, I let resentment rush through me, making my heart beat faster and my stomach feel strange. Did she think she was better than me? I looked at all the pictures of her on my phone because I missed her, but also because she had taken something from me. It was hard to define her particular aesthetic, the vibe she gave off, but whatever you might call it I knew she'd got it from the book.

I subscribed to her channel and turned the notifications on. I watched her videos the moment she uploaded them. They had titles like paintings – *Still Life with Tree Branch*, *Still Life with Dappled Light*. I liked to see the comments come rolling in. Some people didn't understand her project, but there were many others who were intrigued, who found themselves wanting to be like her. *Thank you for your love and light*, they wrote. *Thank you for sharing your dance with nature.* Often, the words were followed by heart emojis, tree emojis, prayer hands. *You are the embodiment of warmth and acceptance. Your work is helping me to heal.* There were other kinds of reactions, too. *Bet u r gr888 in Bed,* said ShavenMark. Bri45 sent three hot dog emojis. *I'M SO CALM NOW*, someone called imnotmartin wrote in multiple comments. *I'M SO CALM. I'M SO CALM. HA I'M NOT.*

When she had made a few dozen videos, she was spotted by an American wellness influencer with over half a million subscribers and an impressive array of product endorsements. Her name was Aspen Smith. She was a tanned, skinny, white woman whose own content often showed her wiping gem stones over her cheekbones or preparing unusual citrus fruits. Aspen Smith had posted a short and chatty vlog in which she talked about other accounts that were inspiring to her, while smearing a mask of whipped avocado over her face. *Still Life* came in at number three. Overnight, she acquired thousands of new followers. She built a website and set up a mailing list. She dabbled in merch. First there were branded T-shirts, locally printed tote bags, and later, a range of scented candles with garden centre names. *Geranium Morning. Birch Light. Eidolic Greens.* Sometimes I thought about buying something. Would she recognise the address? Would she be the person to package the item, to label the box, to write a note? But I didn't want a constant reminder of her rejection, the bag hanging on the coat hook, the candle sitting unused on a bedside table. I wanted to be close to her instead.

On some days, I felt proud of my role in her success. She had made a new life for herself and I had given her some of the tools. I had helped her see herself in a new way, to know that it would be possible to become someone else. On other days, I felt resentful. I still couldn't believe she had abandoned me. I created anonymous accounts and left aggressive comments on her posts. I told her I hated her, that she was hideous, a parasite, and that she ought to feel ashamed. There was nothing to link me to these posts, but I felt sure that she would know that some of them came from me.

For a while, I was locked in this cycle. I was in love with her, then I hated her, then I tried to forget about her completely, then life felt empty and I missed her and I started to love her all over again. But then there came a shift in her content which triggered an important shift in me too. She released a video called *Still Life with Calathea*. In the description box, she offered some advice. *Do you really need the people in your life,* she wrote, *or do they need you? Cut yourself off,* she suggested. *Say goodbye.* At first, I thought she was being hypocritical. I thought: *But you need all of us looking at you.* In a wave of rage, I unsubscribed from everything. I deleted her previous emails. I avoided the internet altogether. I had been working, but it didn't matter. I couldn't concentrate anyway. I spent less and less time in the flat. I walked the fringes of the city. I passed the pleasant suburbs and the less pleasant suburbs and I found myself in the countryside, a long way from home. Then I turned around and walked all the way back, and I understood what I had to do.

Now, I can see things for what they really were. Our relationship was transactional. I gave something to her; she gave something to me. Right at the beginning of her big project, when she didn't yet know what she would become, I validated her process. Likewise, she provided something I sorely needed, though I wasn't much aware of it at the time. She put me in touch with parts of myself that I'd forgotten. She made me feel things again. I had started to love her, which itself was miraculous. I hadn't known I was capable of that. Then I lost her, which felt like hell. But I had remembered how to be vulnerable, and how sometimes it's good to feel pain. These days, there's no more resentment. We are equals. I've learned from her. Some of her followers are real fanatics – they talk about her like she's some kind of god. I'm not like that; I see the performance, the careful staging, the light. But because I really knew her, I have a deeper sense of what she wants to say. Whether she knows it or not, we are closer now than ever before. I'm becoming more and more like her, drawing her spirit into myself.

II

BELLA

One

My daughter once told me she hated her name. 'Okay,' I said calmly. I always tried to be calm with her – she had not asked to be part of this world and did not owe me anything. 'What would you like to be called?' In the weeks and months that followed, we tried on this name, then that. Each one seemed right for a short time. She committed to it fully, then, as quickly as it had come to suit her, she outgrew it and moved on. She'd suggest something else, or she wouldn't, and we would avoid using names for a while. If I was *mama*, she reasoned, then she could be *daughter, child, girl.*

There were other transformations, too. As a teenager, she would come downstairs with her hair arranged in a new way, with eye make-up contoured to change the shape of her whole face. She wore tight, stretchy T-shirts and leggings, exposing the shapes and shadows of her body with less mystery than if she were naked; or she wore huge, diaphanous dresses that threatened to slip from her shoulders, held in place by safety pins or a monkish rope belt. Depending on her mood, she could move differently, smell differently. She could make words sound different in her mouth. She'd tell me about her plans – which friends she was seeing, what time she'd be home – and though the parts of her life were familiar, I'd have the feeling of talking to a stranger. It was as if she could step out of one life and resume another on a parallel track.

Her reinventions had implications for me, too. Sometimes, she played a version of life where she needed a mother like me. At other times, it was as if she were an orphan and that my role was something else: secretary, moneylender, spectator. At best, I felt convenient; at worst, disposable. Each time she became a new person, I was also reconfigured. These days, she has screen names, account names, aliases. Some parts of her life are lived entirely in public; the rest, she keeps to herself.

Two

Recently, she appeared in the colour supplement of a Sunday paper. There was a full-page photograph, a still from a video she had posted, alongside an article about solitude in the modern world. The image was striking and beautiful. In it, she appeared extraordinarily tall and strong. Her gaze fell, as it usually did, just above the camera lens so that, for a moment, you might think she was looking straight at you, but in fact she was looking through you to something beyond. I kept the magazine for a long time. I left it open on the kitchen table. I looked at her while I ate my cereal in the mornings, while I boiled pasta at night. The article was full of dictionary definitions, separating solitude from loneliness, privacy from isolation. It complained, abstractly, about depressed teenagers playing video games. It cited an out-of-context statistic about the way we talk, or don't talk anymore, to other people on the street. It referenced a video my daughter had posted, from which the still was taken, and it quoted some text from the description box in which she claimed to need no one, only herself.

Aesthetically, this particular video wasn't much different to her others. It featured her usual lengthy meditation, overlaid with flutes and wind chimes. In the foreground was a large and veiny calathea plant, while the garden behind her provided a satisfying textural backdrop – a lilac spray of Russian sage, a japonicus bush with leaves like coins. By contrast, her body appeared smooth and polished. There were catch-lights in her eyes. Her skin glowed and her hair came down around her face in glassy waves. She had filmed at sundown. The light was perfect, shifting subtly over the duration. The journalist reported how many times the video had been viewed and shared, and how many people had been moved to comment. Her regular viewers praised her for her beauty and her strength. Aggressive newcomers made sexually explicit comments about her body. Some were offended by her claim to self-sufficiency, by her rejection of community, but there were others who took her at her word. Inspired by her commitment to solitude and selfhood, these followers began to make plans of their own. In forums and threads, they proposed new ways to live, each more extreme, more isolated, than the last. They would move to the countryside and sell their television sets. They would filter the noise of the internet with clever, content-blocking apps so that their only sources of information would be wholesome and pure. They would ghost their friends, shun their families, abandon their places of work. The social structures of their lives would disintegrate and give way. This loss would make space for freedom. On the other side, there would be tranquillity.

In the video's caption box, my daughter elaborated her position. Isolation, she said, was essential for creative growth. She linked to other accounts that celebrated solitude, often coining new words, such as *lonefulness* and *alonement*. She wrote about spiritual leaders who found enlightenment in silence, she wrote about artists who withdrew from the world for the good of their craft. She referenced an exhibition I'd held when she was still young – a series of paintings of the backs of people's heads. *Aloneness can be beautiful*, she wrote. These were the only kinds of interactions she tolerated now – citations and remembered conversations, things she could fold into her philosophy without ever having to confront the complexity of another human being.

Three

The article mentioned my website. That was how another mother came to write to me. The mother's message was long and detailed, the language awkward and detached. *I am writing about your daughter on the internet. I assume you know what she's up to on there.* It was not as accusatory as it might have been – she built her petitions on common ground.

Speaking as one mother to another ...

As a parent, you're bound to feel ...

Her son, she told me, had disappeared. For a while, they had maintained contact, though she no longer knew where he was. Now, she hadn't heard from him in weeks. He had stopped working. She'd been to his flat and seen the heap of unpaid bills, the untouched surfaces of the kitchen, the sour milk in the fridge. She feared for his future, for what would become of his former life should he choose to return to it one day. She had begged him to think carefully, not to throw it all away, but the more she pleaded, the more remote he had become. Towards the end of the message, she told me to make my daughter stop. I considered this for some time. She had asked her own grown-up child to change course to no avail. What responsibility did I have? Legally, and perhaps morally, my daughter's actions were her own, though no parent is comforted by that. I considered the circumstances of my daughter's upbringing, how quiet it had been, how few people we knew, but to understand her, now, as the logical consequence of her childhood made me uncomfortable – not just because I would be forced, again, to confront my own failures, but because it undermined her agency. Often, it had seemed to me that the real authority lay with her, that she had always been in charge, and that all I had ever done was respond.

Four

My father died while I was pregnant. I was twenty-nine years old. It was one of the coldest winters on record. He was cold and alone and the phone lines were down. It took the neighbours a long time to reach me. Eventually a note – which did not say he was dead but implied as much in its urgency – arrived in a pale green envelope. I went to him. There were arrangements and flowers, administration and gifts of food. He – which meant I – received a lot of post. The snow let off for a few days and I kept my antenatal appointments. Then the snow started up again and the funeral was moved back by a week. I remember the funeral director's apologies on the phone. They had never been so busy, he explained. I remember calling around to pass on the new date, how some people seemed terribly inconvenienced by the change. *This is all rather last-minute, wouldn't you say? What's a bit of snow?* All the while, I stayed in my father's house and the neighbours were kind to me. They brought cakes and stews. Old ladies offered strange but good-natured advice when I passed them in the street. *Try putting lard on your toast to keep the baby warm. Always wear a silken cap in bed.*

After the funeral, people said: *So good about the baby. So good to have something to look forward to.* At night in bed, my heart beat quickly. My legs trembled, pumped full of adrenaline, and the baby, soaking up the bad hormones, kicked and squirmed. There was much to do and no one to help. I had no siblings. My mother walked out when I was young – I hadn't seen her for many years. For the first time, I was truly alone, not by choice but by circumstance.

I had many strange dreams. I dreamt my mother was having a baby and I had to get her to hospital. I dreamt that I myself had died and that water was flowing over me. In the middle of the night, I tried, feverishly, to land on a specific memory of my father, but the images rising up were generic and vague. I saw him doing the things he'd always done, at forty, at fifty, at sixty, and found myself unable to remember distinctly the many different people he must have been. He'd had his routines, his meals, his many plants, his nightly whisky and his sad Russian novels. I couldn't remember with any precision the last time I had spoken to him because so many of our conversations were the same. He would tell me he had nothing to say, that nothing had happened, and then embark upon a meandering recollection about the garden, about the book he was reading, about going for a walk. *I saw Mrs Nolan at the grocer's,* he might say. *She was wearing her husband's coat again. She waved to me, or at least I think she was waving to me, and I put the cauliflower into the basket in order that I might wave back. The light was a little hazy, perhaps some dust from the delivery they'd had,* and so on. He loved the details of life, the minutiae. He loved to observe without being seen. He had no desire to prove himself and no audience that might demand such proof. During our telephone calls, he narrated the events of his day as though it were up to me to locate the moments of real significance.

Five

I couldn't live in my father's house for long. His quiet life, his scant belongings, had been beautifully curated. I didn't want to fill his home with my art materials and paintings, with half a lifetime's worth of diaries and all the vanity of my creative ambitions. I gave away his things, keeping only the books and a few shirts that were large enough to hold my pregnant body. I sold the house for less than its true value to a nice couple at the beginning of their retirement, because they admired the way my father had arranged his vegetable patch. With my inheritance, I bought a small stone house in the countryside beneath a railway track. I moved in three weeks before she was born, then we lived there together, my daughter and I, for eighteen years.

The house was nestled snug into the bank of the railway line. From the exterior it appeared large but the walls were so thick that, once inside, it felt small and dark. The ceilings were low and beamed. A wide wooden door opened directly into the kitchen, where the walls were a pale blue and paint crumbled around the window frames. The previous owners had left behind some hotchpotch furniture: a throne-like dark-wood chair, an oak dining table, a leather wing-backed Chesterfield and an iron chandelier with candle-flame bulbs that were impossible to replace. The kitchen floor was laid with deep-red tiles, badly cracked. There were gaps in the woodchip wallpaper, clefts where the plaster showed beneath. I never did anything to it, no redecoration, no repairs. Rather, I left it as I found it, and there was freedom in that. I marvelled at it sometimes, the way you might marvel at something in nature. *What a vibrant shade of green inside the wardrobe doors. What elegant curves in the garden railings.* It seemed to me that nothing there was our fault, that the house did not truly belong to us, but that we had only borrowed it for a time. When I lit the open fire in winter, a small patch of brick would warm above the mantel. Otherwise, the house was impervious to us.

A low arch connected the kitchen to the hall, which in turn led to the living room, the study, the downstairs lavatory and the stairs. The back part of the house was always dark, half submerged in the garden, which rose up the bank towards the tracks. The garden itself was large, an irregularly shaped lawn with overgrown flower beds and large bushes carving out alcoves and hidden corners. There were stone steps where the bank became steeper and where the previous owners had dug out two tiers. The first was paved with stone slabs, the second grassed over and barely deep enough to stand. A single imposing tree stood in the middle of the lawn. When she was older, my daughter liked to sit on the higher ledges of the garden and watch the birds among the leaves. Sometimes, I'd look out of the bedroom window and see her through the branches and it was as if she had floated up there.

The study was lined on three walls with deep bookshelves. There was a couch I never sat on, and a chair where I liked to read. I bought a desk when my daughter was four and started school, but only ever used it a handful of times. It was an imposing antique thing with delicate marquetry and gold-handled drawers. I'd kept journals since I was a girl. I needed somewhere to put them, and I wanted a beautiful place to write – as if the act of recording my life, and in turn the life itself, would become more valuable. But the desk was too grandiose and the business of writing too absurd. When I wrote, I sat on the floor, propped up with cushions and draped in scarves like an ancient statue.

Upstairs, there was one large bedroom, and a small narrow room with a single bed. We shared the larger room until she was nine years old. Sometimes it felt as if we lived our whole lives there. We kept our clothes in one large wardrobe with a mirror in the door. We dressed and undressed in front of it, becoming our various selves. Lying in bed at night, she would confide in me, telling me things that happened at school that were easier to say when the lights were out. If I had a new project, I would sketch in bed before taking the idea to the studio. Sometimes she sat in bed with me, with a sketchbook of her own. There were days when this filled me with joy, and days when it filled me with rage. I had no space of my own. I was sick of her touch, her weight against me, her loud breathing, her watery eyes, the way she wriggled and trembled and squirmed. She treated me like furniture, I thought. Like something she might rearrange on a whim.

She lives there now, without me. It has all been turned over to her.

Six

I don't know that I loved my daughter right away. As they handed her to me in the hospital, there was an abundance of sensation, too much for one person to hold. The physical afterpains of birth did not, as I had been told, disappear the moment she lay in my arms. As I looked at her, I felt the full extent of the evacuation: the hollowness and blood loss, the tearing and wrenching of the gut. She weighed only five pounds. Her limbs were fragile, strange and birdlike. She was so still that it wasn't until I heard her scream that I knew she was alive. I fed her the sticky yellow substance that appears before the milk. She drank it and threw up, not just the yellow stuff but all kinds of waters and phlegms. We spent three days on the ward. The midwives were reluctant to let me go. They asked me again and again what family I had, who would help me with the baby. It was as if, by keeping me there, they thought my answer might improve.

In the middle of the night, she would look up at me and I would trace the strange, round shape of her mouth and watch it tremble as she cried. She was glorious and terrifying, and I thought: who made this? There was an instinctive bond between us, so predetermined, so primal, that I couldn't trust it. I had not chosen it, and so I felt hijacked, unmoored in a world where I had no father, no parents, but this small damp creature, a pinkish shape in my arms. When she settled, I'd place her in the centre of the bed and curl myself around her like a giant parenthesis. I'd listen to her breathing and think: *there is a stranger in my bed.*

At first, it was only a half-love – something animal and bodily that refused to align with my conscious mind. But slowly, other kinds of love emerged. She made beautiful, gentle sounds, unconstrained by language or thought. She was strong and she was curious. She loved to be in the garden, to feel the textures of grass and leaves. When I waved toys in front of her, she looked at them but did not reach out. She often sighed. At seven weeks old, she started smiling, though never at me. She smiled at shifts in the light, the shadows of branches on the ceiling, at the movements of her own, tiny hands. Through observing her, I came to love her differently, with mind and body together. I knew who she was, I thought, so I could love her consciously. There followed a period of deep contentment. In meeting her needs, in surrendering my body to her, I was, for a short time, entirely satisfied. We lived in the deep quiet of the old stone house, hearing the trains go by, seeing no one, doing nothing but keeping ourselves alive.

In the evenings, once she had gone to sleep, I would listen to music and draw freely. I filled sketchbook after sketchbook with wild, incoherent things. There was no purpose to it. I didn't recognise my own style, which was liable to change from one day to the next. Some of the drawings were very bad and I didn't care. I often thought of the midwives asking me nervously who was going to help me, and I thought how disorientating it would have been to have a child with someone else. I was glad to be on my own, an orphan with a baby. I was free to adapt to her needs. I was the only one to truly know her; she had all my attention. I gave to her, and I got from her, all my love.

Seven

At nursery, she changed. My calm, solid baby, who knew what she wanted and how to ask for it, became fearful and volatile. Big feelings rose within her and spilled out, too much for her body to hold. The brief period where I felt that I had known her was, I realised, a fiction. She was formless, inconsistent. I had no idea who she was.

She screamed as I drove the winding tree-lined road between our village and the town. As I lifted her from the car seat, she pulled violently at her hair.

'I'll stay with you,' I tried to comfort her. 'Until you feel ready to play.'

She kicked and thrashed and hit her head against my knees. When I picked her up, she clawed my neck. Once, she bit herself hard on the wrist, leaving deep, glistening imprints. After a while, she would exhaust herself, at which point I passed her over to the nursery staff, who gave me pitiful looks.

'She isn't like this at home,' I told them, but I saw they didn't believe it, and soon enough it ceased to be true.

When I picked her up at the end of the day, they would narrate to me the various strategies by which she had avoided other children and refused her food. *She barricaded herself behind the doll's house. She spat her breadsticks into the sandpit. She hid pasta in the shape sorter. She lay face down on the floor for an hour.* The only activity she seemed to enjoy was *outside chalk*, where she drew long tendril-like shapes across the tarmac then swept them away with warm water and a little baby mop. She'd nap in the car on the way home, then on her play mat in the living room. I'd wake her for dinner, which she ate quickly, then she went to bed, where she slept as if dead. She became scared of many things: the darkened spaces beneath tables and chairs, the shadowy triangles behind open doors, letter boxes, plugholes, radiator vents. In the middle of the night, she would wake and be furious with me for turning off the lights. Fear and anger were her primary languages. They moved through her body and took hold.

At first, it was a subtle thing, a restless shudder or a twitch in her leg, but later her whole body shook. I found myself unable to ease her, looking on at what seemed to me like a slow-motion electrocution. Something had invaded her. As though fighting infection, she was trying to sweat and shiver it out. At nursery, the other parents were unsettled by her anxious body while their children tried to make it behave. I saw toddlers pin her arms to her sides and sit on her legs to make them still. Eventually, I stopped taking her there. I told myself it was the social environment that had made her anxious, that she was too sensitive to the feelings and urges of other children. But even if this diagnosis were correct, it was too late. She did not return to stillness.

She fidgeted constantly, jiggling her legs and feet, or tapping her hands on my arm. When she wasn't trembling, she was flicking something, shifting around in her chair, picking maniacally at the hem of a dress or pulling out strand after strand of her hair. She dropped things, broke things, tripped over nothing. It didn't seem to be a lack of spatial awareness so much as a discomfort with space itself. At night, I hummed to her and held her. I stroked her head. As she drifted off, I listened to her breath become soft and small while her hands opened and closed around the air. When she was quiet like this, I was peaceful. To soothe her was to succeed. I wanted to believe I could conquer her ailments, I could meet her every need. That was the beginning of my confusion. For the next few years, I didn't know if my primary desire to make her well was founded in her best interests or in mine.

Eight

Her favourite jumper had a little pocket shaped like a whale, her favourite toy was a purple-haired rag doll named *Dragon*. When we drew pictures, she took her time over the details. She examined her subjects carefully, tracing the edges with a finger, before committing her crayon to the page. She kept her legs folded neatly beneath her, which stilled their trembling awhile. I took her to see various doctors who all said that the shaking would pass. They watched her sitting on my knee. They'd see the shudder that started in one foot and travelled upwards into her body and shoulders. They saw how the movement ebbed and flowed so that, when the shaking was at its strongest, I shook too. They ran a lot of tests. She wasn't suffering from seizures or low blood pressure; she did not have any other symptoms alongside which a tremor would usually present. What appeared to confound, and later irritate, them the most was that her behaviour was not consistent.

Sometimes she shook violently, sometimes there was only a light twitch in her hands. Sometimes she was perfectly still. Nobody said outright that she might just be making it up, but the implication was often there, along with a note of judgement. *And why might she feel the need to do that?* There were specialists in London, I was told. *A postcode lottery.* We were sent to a child psychologist in Sheffield, but no clear diagnosis was offered.

'She doesn't get enough sleep,' the psychologist said.

'No, she doesn't,' I replied, which left us at an impasse of cause and effect.

For me, the tragedy was not that she shook, but that often this was the only thing other people noticed about her. They didn't know that she was headstrong, imaginative, independent. They didn't see that she was good at drawing, that she liked to do cartwheels and backward bends, that she tucked her hair into her collar when she ate, that she knew the names of a great many shades of green. At primary school, her classmates kept their distance. Her first teacher tried not to draw attention to her. There was a classroom assistant who asked her repeatedly what was wrong, or if something very bad had happened to her. She told me about it after school because it weighed on her. *What kind of bad thing does she mean? What should I say?* I advised her to tell the truth, which made her cry. It was a ridiculous thing for me to have said: she didn't know the truth of it. Neither did I.

Those days were sheltered and repetitive. Time passed quickly, though nothing ever seemed to change. I saw very few people. I took her to school, I cleaned and shopped. In the afternoons I painted, mechanically and without urgency. I produced work steadily, without any particular desire to do it. I learned that one way of being creative is simply to negotiate the things you can't do. For a while, faces were impossible. When I painted them, they felt untrue, so I gave up and painted only the backs of people's heads.

Once every few weeks, her teacher would pull me aside after school. *I'm afraid she's had a bad day. I'm afraid today has been a struggle.* I wondered at the teacher's inability to describe it in literal terms: she trembled, she could not be still. The teacher would go on. *Perhaps there's something playing on her mind. Is everything all right at home? Would it be helpful for us to speak with her father?* The tone of the questions shifted from one conversation to the next. Sometimes it was sympathetic; sometimes impatient, accusatory, sad. I tried to be consistent in my responses. *She's doing her best. We're trying something new.*

There were many clinics and experts, each fluent in their own field and uncomprehending of any other. We saw specialists in nutrition, mental health, Traditional Chinese Medicine, homeopathy, reiki, psychotherapy, osteopathy, medicinal dance. At every appointment, a new methodology was described to us in detail. *This is our approach, here's what's going to happen next, and here's what to expect for next time.* There were booklets and lollipops and complimentary teas. There was so much preparation and procedure, it was as if there would never be time for a cure. The appointments were exhausting. Each process was long and formal and required us to educate ourselves, in biology, neurology, Eastern philosophy. We learned how energy moved through the body, the location of the chakras and which among them were blocked. We practised therapeutic chants. Each time we began again, we were hopeful and curious, wide-eyed and nodding as the various systems were explained to us. An hour later, when we were at home and she was shaking more than before, disappointment would set in, the familiar feeling of inevitability.

I was often aware of how strange we must have seemed to others – teachers and doctors, the other parents at the school gates. Sometimes, I tried to imagine how we might appear to a stranger, if someone were to watch us together at home. There was the shaking daughter whose trembling, if it were the plot of a film, would have to be caused by some form of possession, an evil spirit. And then there was me, the myopic mother, so entirely consumed by the day-to-day that I couldn't see the greater dangers encroach. There is something about looking after a small child, the child's insistence on the present, that is like living in a horror movie: you're trapped in peaceful ignorance, forever distracted by menial tasks, while the audience looks on with a sense of foreboding. They know that, in the chaos of the moment, you'll fail to see the real danger ahead.

Nine

Soon, she was the tallest in her class. There were a lot of growing pains. Not the metaphorical ones, but the literal, bone-aching, muscle-expanding, skin-stretching sensations of a body getting larger. Sometimes, she would moan in this awful, gurning way and describe her various aches. It was as if I could feel the pain in my own bones and muscles, or at least the shadow of it, a mimetic sensation in an arm or a leg. Her teachers complained that she often made strange noises – low and guttural, animal sounds. It was distracting for the other children, they said. *It made it hard for them to focus.* The whole matter of putting a child through school seemed to me a strange experiment in teaching children what kinds of things would be rewarded with attention, or not. For some children, a neat painting or a clever joke, an unerring sum or a good throw would earn you a moment of acknowledgement. For others, it would be a rude word or a playground shove. For my daughter, it was always her body. When she was shaking, people noticed; when she was still, they did not.

There was one teacher she loved dearly – Miss Tamm, who was tall and solid-looking, like an expensive piece of furniture. She had a square face and a large straight mouth which gave her a permanently serious expression. At first, I liked her too. She reminded me a little of myself, unmarried and independent. She was practical and kind, not easily spooked by trembling limbs and juddering speech. In the manner of a therapist, she made neutral observations. *I notice that your arm is shaking today. How do you feel about that?* When she entered Miss Tamm's class, my daughter was nine, but looked much older. She had small breasts, a noticeable roundness at her hips. Her features had subtly reconfigured so that, in the duration of a glance, she might resemble a sullen teenager and then, without warning, become a little girl again.

She got her first period that year. The stain on her skirt was hardly more than a speck, but it was enough for Miss Tamm to notice and whisk her aside as the other children stood in line for playtime. Miss Tamm informed me of this at the school gates, skilfully separating me from the other parents and delivering the news in determinedly scientific, non-euphemistic language. My daughter had begun *menstruation*, had been provided with the *relevant sanitary materials*. She had also been given a key to the teachers-only room, where the bathroom had the right kind of bin.

'Do any other students use it?' I asked.

Miss Tamm said that she was the only one.

At home, she showed me the little pouch Miss Tamm had bestowed upon her: three pads, a panty liner, an informative leaflet with diagrams. According to the leaflet, periods were purple while ovaries were pink with smiley faces. According to the leaflet, she would get used to her periods after a couple of months. I was unconvinced by this. I never remembered when my period was due. I experienced the bleeding as an affront, an unwelcome reminder that my body was never truly within my control. Over the course of my life, I had tried to reclaim it with various medical interventions. For a while, I had lived with an intrauterine device, a T-shaped copper object for decapitating sperm, until I started having recurring dreams that it was moving around my body, that somehow it had made its way inside my organs where it roamed freely, according to its will. I didn't tell the doctor this when I asked to have it removed. I simply said that it was painful and, during the appointment, he acted as though he were doing it all out of some great favour to me, as if it wasn't my right to decide what lived inside me or did not. When I was an art student, I had tried going on the pill. It had the bizarre effect of making me both cripplingly sad and insufferably self-aggrandising at once. My work was terrible, I thought. My education was futile, I had no potential. I was the *most* talentless, the *most* mediocre student ever to have enrolled. I stopped going to lectures, instead spending my days reading magazines and imagining all the terrible things the other students thought about me. When my father pointed out that – as I had attended so little of the first semester – they most likely didn't think of me at all, I sobbed. When at last I stopped taking the pill, my life seemed new and hopeful. I could concentrate again. I read everything I had missed. I discovered oils and learned the proper techniques. For a few years, I was filled with a bright and infectious energy. I drew good people towards me. Anything I needed, I could conjure for myself. Unregulated menstruation seemed a fair price to pay for that kind of power. The only time that I had not suffered from either my periods or their cure was during pregnancy. But after my daughter was born, once I stopped breastfeeding and bleeding resumed, it was worse than ever before. I got blinding headaches and terrible cramps, a scraping feeling in the gut that over-the-counter painkillers couldn't touch.

I assumed that my daughter would feel embarrassed, maybe even ashamed, the way I had experienced my first period, terrified that other people would know that something was happening to me. Or else, I expected her to feel the way I felt about my nine-year-old girl suffering monthly pains and bleeds: as if her childhood had been unfairly cast aside. But she felt none of these things. She was pleased, a little smug, as though in possession of an important secret.

'Were you scared?' I asked her in the car.

'Miss Tamm says it's perfectly normal.'

I tried to read her expression, neutral or pointed. 'It is perfectly normal,' I said.

'Actually, Miss Tamm was quite shocked that I didn't know what it was.' She looked at me through narrowed eyes.

'Did Miss Tamm explain it to you?'

'Yes,' she said. 'I know everything now.' She paused, then added: 'Miss Tamm took excellent care of me.'

The steering wheel felt soft and light beneath my hands – flimsy, as though it might turn this way or that with the slightest touch. My right foot trembled, I wasn't sure which pedal it touched. As we approached a red light, the car accelerated violently before I hit the brake and stalled. We lurched forwards. I felt her eyes on me.

'What's wrong with you?' she said, sounding just like an adult.

'I slipped,' I told her. 'I'm sorry.'

'Miss Tamm would say you need to calm down,' she said. 'Miss Tamm would tell you to take a deep breath.'

I knew that she wanted to shame me. I knew I had not done my job. She was still so young; I had thought there would be more time. But the more I considered it, the larger the failing became. It wasn't just that I hadn't told her, it was that I had taken some trouble to conceal the evidence of my own periods, storing and disposing of the necessary materials so that she would never find them. It had not been a conscious decision – I had simply done what felt natural to me. In how many other ways, I wondered, had I unknowingly failed her? I pictured the future: a dismal corridor of revelations, each more damning than the one before.

At home, I asked her if she was in pain and she said no. I asked if she had any particular feelings about what had happened. She said she didn't think so, but she'd let me know if anything changed. She understood her power over me, that I had been exposed.

'I should have told you,' I said. 'I'm sorry.'

She paused, playing with the hem of her skirt and pulling lightly at a broken seam. 'It doesn't matter,' she said. 'Miss Tamm was there.'

That evening, she demanded a hot-water bottle for her cramps because Miss Tamm had said it would help.

'I thought you weren't in pain,' I said.

'It's just started,' she whimpered. 'It's awful.'

'Where does it hurt?'

She rubbed her hands the length of her torso, from the top of her ribcage to her hip bones. 'Miss Tamm said it might be like this.'

'Why don't you go upstairs and lie down,' I told her. 'I'll bring the hot-water bottle to you.'

My own periods had started late, at seventeen. Perhaps I should have suspected that she would be different. In physical terms, we had never been much alike: me, taking after my father, small-boned and wan; her favouring my mother, strong and broad. I boiled the water and made up the bottle.

Upstairs, I found her on the floor of the small room, lying in the narrow gap between the door and the bed. When she saw me, she made a great show of sitting up. Her arms trembled at her sides. Her legs shook lightly. She was pale. I gave her the bottle. She held it to her midriff and reclined dramatically, in the manner of a Victorian lady upon a fainting couch.

'Wouldn't you be more comfortable on the big bed?' I asked her.

'I need privacy.' She sighed and closed her eyes.

I tried to remember when I had learned about periods, or what I'd done when I got my own. Who had I told? My father? A friend? My mother was gone by then. Did someone help me? Had I already known what to do? I only remembered embarrassment, and a sick, hot feeling. No one had made me feel important or cared for, or that I understood anything about womanhood.

There were many things that my mother had never done for me that I had vowed to do for my daughter, in reparation. My mother had never seen any of my paintings; I hung all of her artwork on the kitchen wall. My mother never heard me talk about what I wanted to do when I grew up; I took her future plans, even the most outlandish ones, very seriously. Still, I had left her unprepared. I considered my threshold for failure. I sensed that it was low. Then I thought of Miss Tamm, who knew nothing about me, but who appeared to delight in my incompetence: a woman who loved to see another woman fail.

Ten

In October, Miss Tamm told the class that she was pregnant. Each night when she came home, my daughter described to me the changes to her teacher's body, noting shifts in the colour of her cheeks, the size of her ankles and the fact that when she was hot you could see it in her neck. *Miss Tamm has a special chair, now. She sits with her legs wide apart. Her hair is bigger, curlier than before. When Miss Tamm wears her tight beige dress, we can see the baby when it moves.* She asked me a lot of questions about the unborn child: how big it might be and how the doctors would know if something went wrong with it. I'd given her dolls to play with, but she had never taken much interest in them. She preferred utilitarian toys, things she could make and build and do. I was puzzled by her fascination with the baby, until I understood that she saw it as a threat.

'What if the baby gets too big?' she asked. 'What if the

baby takes something from Miss Tamm's body that she needs for herself? What if Miss Tamm doesn't like the baby when it comes?'

There were questions, too, about the mechanics of childbirth. In biology books, we looked at peach-coloured cross sections of pregnant bodies. She wanted to know about my experience and I said, truthfully, that giving birth was the strangest, wildest joy I'd ever felt. But that was too abstract for her. She wanted specific details, and there were many things I couldn't recall. I told her it had happened quickly, without pain relief, a long time ago. She was frustrated, perhaps offended, by the gaps in my memory, as if I hadn't been paying proper attention. She asked me if Miss Tamm's baby had a father and I told her I didn't know.

'Sometimes I think you and Miss Tamm are just the same,' she said.

'Oh?'

'And other times you're completely different. Then I think Miss Tamm is more like me.'

'Is that so,' I said. It was the weekend. We were having breakfast at the large oak table. She was sipping a cup of warm milk, holding it firmly in both hands so that her trembling wouldn't make it spill.

'If something awful happens to you one day,' she said, 'I think I'd like to go and live with Miss Tamm.'

'Good for you,' I said. I brought my coffee cup to my lips with one hand, picked up a slice of honeyed toast with the other.

'I mean, if you were in a car accident. Or if you got really ill and couldn't function anymore. If you did something stupid, like burned down the house while you were asleep.'

'Do you worry about those things?'

'Not worry,' she said. 'They're like stories I play in my head.'

'Fantasies.'

'No, stories.'

'And in these stories, you think Miss Tamm would want to live with you?'

She remained calm, a little superior. 'Miss Tamm likes me,' she said. 'She likes me more than the other children. She told me.'

'She said it just like that? *I like you more than the other children?*'

'Pretty much.'

I suggested that it wasn't very professional of Miss Tamm to say something like that. 'What about the others?' I said. 'Wouldn't their feelings be hurt if they knew?'

She laughed. 'I'm just saying that Miss Tamm loves me.' She put down her milk. I sipped more coffee. She shook wildly in her seat. 'She can't help it. She loves me just like a mother would.'

She was watching me intently. I offered her some toast and she refused.

The rest of the day was difficult. Everything she wanted to do – drawing, dancing, dressing up, reading, practising cartwheels on the lawn – ended in a confrontation with her shaking body. I made her favourite foods for dinner – pasta with sage butter, wilted spinach, bread pudding – but still she didn't eat. That night, it took a long time for her to fall asleep. She was hungry and agitated. Her limbs would not rest. We read stories. I sang to her, as I had when she was a baby. I held her tightly and stroked her hair.

'Picture yourself in a safe and peaceful place,' I said, hoping she would be kind enough not to tell me where she'd gone: Miss Tamm's house or Miss Tamm's garden, or walking on a beautiful beach with Miss Tamm. As a girl, I had found it thrilling to imagine myself into other families – to pretend I belonged to my friends' parents, or to glamorous-looking women I saw in the street. I fantasised about my teachers taking me home or falling in love with my father and then coming to live with us, transforming our house into something hopeful and new. Sometimes, I fantasised about my father's disappearance so that I might be given to a family that felt complete. It didn't seem unnatural to me for a child to dream about their parents disappearing. Most children's stories relied upon the absence of caregivers in order for the children to do anything. But I wanted very badly to be my daughter's sole protector; I wanted her to need me in that way. Sometimes, this was my greatest desire, even greater than my desire for her to be well.

Eleven

In the weeks leading up to Miss Tamm's maternity leave, my daughter became angry and cruel. She told me directly that everything wrong with her was my fault. It was my responsibility to help her, so why had I not? I was not a good mother, she said. I did nothing for her, I had no use. The more she committed herself to this argument, the worse her condition became. She begged me to call the consultants and therapists we'd seen before. Some of them added her to their waiting lists, which they assured me were very long; others wanted to know if she would truly commit herself to a cure this time, as though my nine-year-old's physical and emotional well-being were simply a question of good mental attitude. We were both exhausted. Neither of us was sleeping. She woke me up in the early hours, terrified that she would never get better. She would cry and say how hopeless it all seemed, and then in the morning she felt silly because her body was still and she felt calm. We'd eat our toast with marmalade, drink our tea and juice, and wonder why it had all felt so desperate in the depths of night. But by the time we arrived at school, the shaking would have started again, and the cycle of emotions recommenced. As though her condition were contagious, I became so tired that often my own hands shook. When I tried to focus on the details of things, my vision would blur.

One afternoon, I went to pick her up after netball practice. When I arrived at school, the girls were still playing, their little yellow bibs darting across the court. I squinted against the light and tried to pick her out: my tall, long-limbed daughter who played in defence. The sun was low and blinding, a hot-metal white. I saw nothing distinctly, a blur of colour and shapes against tarmac. Red and black spots drifted and swooped in front of my eyes. I was dizzy, a little nauseous. My head ached. I turned away from the light. In a gesture that was at once alarming and familiar, I thought I saw someone waving at me. I stumbled a little, still struggling to focus. The ground seemed to shift beneath me and, briefly, I returned to my childhood, to my own first school and the sensation of looking for my mother at the end of the day. I was small and overshadowed, peering up at the crowd of bodies, not knowing which hand to grab.

'Hello,' someone was calling to me. 'Are you all right?'

It was Miss Tamm, with one long hand raised. She was sitting in the grassy part of the playground, next to a jungle-themed climbing frame. Her legs were stretched out wide, her back supported by a mouldy-looking wooden pole carved into a palm tree. The sky was a bright and pale grey; a patch of navy in the distance threatened a storm. Miss Tamm appeared larger than ever, with her long limbs splayed and the weight of pregnancy drawing her forwards. There was a flush in her cheeks, her lips were parted. She was breathing heavily through her mouth. It was disarming to see her so relaxed, so soft. Slowly, I went to her. She gestured for me to sit down, so I perched on a crocodile-shaped log.

'You don't look well,' she said.

I tried to sit taller, to tidy my hair behind my ears. 'I'm a little tired.'

Miss Tamm leaned back, propped on her elbows, in a position so open and vulnerable it was almost obscene.

'I've been thinking about your daughter,' she said, waving a nonchalant hand towards the group of girls who were starting to remove their netball bibs.

'Has she done something wrong?' I said. 'She's getting worse, I think.' My head was still throbbing. It was too hot, too light. 'It's my fault,' I said. 'She's not getting any better.'

'Of course it isn't,' Miss Tamm said quickly, without pity or condolence. 'My mother thought everything was her fault, too,' she said. 'I can assure you it never made anything better for me.'

A trestle table had been laid out beside the netball court. The children were drinking cups of juice while the teacher appraised their game.

Miss Tamm said something else I didn't hear clearly.

'I'm sorry?' I said.

'I said I have something that might help.'

From her satchel, she took out a cassette tape and handed it to me. There was no cover and no label. The tape was half wound.

'It's a meditation,' she said.

'We've tried meditation. We've tried all kinds.'

She adjusted her sitting position again, then cracked her neck and rubbed the tops of her arms with her hands. 'Pregnancy is terrible,' she said. 'My back hurts. My hips feel twisted. Everything is swollen, full of water. They say you forget all about it.' She looked at me directly. 'They say that afterwards you only remember the bits that were nice.'

I thought of my own pregnancy – the snow, the power cuts, the house, my father. Pregnancy had been easy, I thought. The circumstances were hard. But still, there had been some sense of liberation in the chaos. I had stopped trying to force the world into a shape I liked. I had finally understood that anything that had happened to someone else was also something that could happen to me. I remembered the hollow feeling I'd had once the baby was no longer inside me, how I'd still felt the shadow of a baby in there, kicking and turning, long after she was born.

'I've been doing breathing exercises to prepare for the birth.' She pointed to the tape in my hands. 'Even if it does no good, it won't do any harm.'

I thought of all the other failed cures, the long list of disappointments. 'I think I liked being pregnant,' I said to Miss

Tamm. 'The feeling of possibility – the feeling that the person inside you could be anyone.'

'Really?' she said, surprised. 'How strange. I feel I already know exactly who she is.'

I stood up. Miss Tamm shifted her weight from side to side. She looked confused. I almost felt sorry for her. I didn't know if she had anyone to help her, or if she was having the baby on her own. I suspected the midwives wouldn't pity her the way they'd pitied me – Miss Tamm was tall, imposing, strong-willed, unflappable. I had been small and weak and shocked.

'It's so hard getting up and down these days,' she said.

I held out my hands.

She gripped them hard. A sharp pain shot through my knuckles and wrists. I was unprepared for the strain on my shoulders as she tried to right herself. I stumbled and she stepped back, and back again, losing her balance. I pictured her falling, her large body hitting the ground, landing awkwardly, painfully, on an animal log – the shock, the bruise, the danger to the unborn child. I steadied myself and held her weight. Miss Tamm groaned and then sighed. She draped a muscular arm around me. The warmth of it was awful. I never touched anyone other than my daughter. The embrace came as a kind of assault. I thought of my mother again. I thought of the friends I'd had in school. My head became light and watery. A hot shiver slipped between my shoulder blades. I thanked her for the tape and said goodbye.

I retrieved my daughter from the tangle of girls. She was

trembling lightly, clutching a bunch of chocolate fingers that were melting in her palm.

'How was practice today?' I asked her in the car.

'What were you talking to Miss Tamm about?' she replied.

'Being pregnant.'

She scowled at me, clearly irritated that I could discuss something with Miss Tamm that she could not. 'Is it good, being pregnant?' she asked.

'It's strange,' I said. 'Your body is no longer your own.'

'You have to share it.'

'Yes.'

'That's terrible.'

'It's lovely, too,' I said. 'Wherever you go, you have someone. A friend.'

She screwed up her face, as she did whenever I said anything sentimental. 'You can't be friends with something not born.'

We drove through the woods between our village and the next, sunlight strobing through the trees. She ate her biscuits, then licked the chocolate from her hands.

'Nothing would want to share my body,' she told me. 'Nothing else could live in there.'

Twelve

I considered what to do with the cassette tape. It wouldn't help her, I was sure of that. We had tried so many kinds of meditations, so many exercises in breathing and visualisation and humming and tapping the meridian points of the body with our fingertips. But it seemed possible that the disappointment of another failed remediation – this time a gift from her favourite teacher – might finally cure her of her obsession with Miss Tamm.

A few days later, I was preparing for an exhibition, sitting on the floor among the cushions and the blankets, trying to write a few words to say at the opening. A square of brilliant light beamed in through the study window. Dust particles floated upwards. Everything was quiet. My daughter was watching a film in the next room with the volume turned low. In spite of the warm weather, she had requested hot chocolate and a heavy quilt. I sipped coffee. I wrote a couple of lines in a notebook. Then there came a sheepish knock at the door. She said she didn't want to be alone, so I went to sit with her for a while. Then she said she wanted to be in the study with me, so I went back to my notebook while she drew pictures at the desk. We were both tense, sick of each other and nowhere else to go.

Without even looking at her, I could feel the tremor coming. It was in her power to change the air around her, to summon new spirits into a room. Soon, she was struggling with her drawing. The pencil still jagged at the paper, but not where she wanted it to go. Her muscles spasmed. Red patches appeared on her arms. I heard the grind of her teeth at the back of her mouth. Her breathing became frantic and short.

I started to speak. It was too late.

She lost control. She screamed. Her legs kicked at the chair, the desk, while her arms pounded the table. She stabbed the crayon right through the drawing and made a sharp dent in the wood beneath. The birds in the garden launched themselves upwards in a single motion, their shadows flitting over the carpet. I dissociated. I looked at her as I would a stranger. I saw her limbs thrashing, heard her cries, and felt nothing. The clouds in the sky looked like cartoon clouds. The light shifted subtly through the room. For one fleeting second our eyes met, and she paused her hysterical dance. Her arms settled and her shoulders softened.

'I'm sorry,' I said, but before the words were out she had resumed her wild movements, and this time, I felt sure they were purposeful: not so much a loss of control but a conscious release.

She pushed over the chair to get her full body weight over the desk, to strike it with greater force. She smashed the pickle jar I used as a penholder, then she opened the desk drawer for the sole purpose of slamming it shut as hard as she could. I attempted to manoeuvre myself between her and the desk by holding one of her arms. She was strong. I tightened my grip. She struck out. I pulled her towards me and she wrenched herself free. For a few moments, we were both still. She stopped trembling and clenched her fists. I stepped back and she hurled herself towards me. She bit me, hard, on the neck.

I pushed her. 'What the hell is wrong with you?' I screamed.

She screamed back that she didn't know. She screamed until her voice cracked and her throat became dry, then she murmured things I couldn't hear, words under her breath, a low, subhuman growl.

I picked up my notebook, walked out of the room and slammed the door.

'Do what you want,' I told her calmly. 'Rip the place to shreds if you like.'

I went to the kitchen and put the kettle on the hob. She snarled a low note that seemed to reverberate through the house. My hands trembled as I poured the boiling water. Somewhere outside, a car radio was playing. There was the sound of a train passing over the tracks. I heard voices across the street. In the notebook, I catalogued the sounds – the boiler lurch, the pipe creak, the fridge buzz, the engine slur.

My daughter started to cry, and I recorded that too. Violent sobs gave way to softer ones. I let it cool and then I drank my tea.

When I went back to the study, her face was blotched and pink. There were deep scratches on her arm. I walked towards the desk and she moved aside for me. I opened the drawer, reached my arm to the back. I imagined her coming at me again, slamming the drawer, breaking my wrist. But she didn't, she stayed where she was.

'Miss Tamm wanted you to have this,' I said, and handed over the tape.

She took it in both hands, sitting down on the tall desk chair.

'What is it?'

'Some sort of meditation.'

'Why did she give it to you?'

'She thought you'd like it.'

'Why didn't she just give it to me?'

'Parents like to know if someone gives their child a gift,' I said. It occurred to me that I ought to have listened to the tape before giving it to her.

She located the cassette player in her bedroom. She brushed her hair and put on clean clothes.

'Where should I listen to it?' she asked sweetly.

'Where would you like to listen to it?'

She moved from the kitchen, to the study, back to the living room. 'Outside,' she said at last.

By the time she had positioned herself on the grassy ledge

at the top of the garden, her body was already quite still. I watched her as she carefully, meticulously, slid the tape from its case and put it into the machine. I saw her close her eyes and roll her shoulders back. She stayed there for more than an hour. It was windy and cold and getting dark. I thought of taking her a blanket or a warm drink, but she appeared content so I let her be.

Most likely, it was not the tape itself that made the difference but the fact of Miss Tamm having given it to her. I had been naive to think she would be disappointed. The strength of her feeling was such that disappointment was impossible: Miss Tamm could do no wrong. When at last she came back inside, it was evening and we were late to eat. Her body was still and her breathing was smooth.

'I feel better,' she told me, and her voice was softer, deeper. She stood taller and straighter than before, with her legs in a wide stance. Her mouth was a resolute straight line. There was a new expression in her eyes, I thought. It was not so much calm as smug.

Thirteen

After that, the periods of calm became longer than the periods of disquiet. She listened to the tape at least once a day. There was nothing particularly special about it – visualisations, breathing exercises, delicate music, long moments of silence. I bought her a satchel to carry the cassette player wherever she went. There were cheap plastic headphones all over the house, spare pairs in every room. She insisted we make a back-up copy, which we did, though the sound quality was terrible – mumbled words and white noise. For years, long after she had left primary school, she would remind me how kind it had been of Miss Tamm to have provided the very thing she needed all along. She speculated that Miss Tamm would be a truly excellent mother, and what a lucky little girl her daughter was. Though I felt the sting of this, I too was grateful. The transformation was so startling, so complete, our life together in the old stone house became peaceful again. It was soothing to me that the evidence of my inadequate mothering was no longer on display.

Around this time, she took up painting. She asked me questions about technique and process. She was fascinated by colour, the way that a flat shade of green, left alone on a blank white canvas, was entirely different to the same shade placed alongside coral or lilac or cobalt blue. There were still days when her body seemed to run away from her, but these episodes were infrequent and, when they came, they were usually short-lived. I recalled the words of one of the child psychologists – she did indeed appear to be *growing out of it*. Or more to the point: she had grown into something else. On bad days, we had a process, a set of emergency protocols to follow. The kinds of treats that other children might receive when they were unwell were reserved for when her body refused to behave. There were ice-cream milkshakes and cheese scones and sour-apple sweets. We'd gather our supplies and make a den in the study with the duvet, the desk and the chair. We'd wrap ourselves in blankets and get much too hot, then sip the milkshakes to cool ourselves down. She loved to be swaddled in fabric. Even when she was sixteen, seventeen, eighteen, she liked to be tucked in at night, or gathered into one of my shawls. When we tired of the den, or when it collapsed, we would move to the sofa and I'd drape her in layer after layer of material until only her face could be seen.

When she was thirteen or fourteen years old, she had a favourite film called *The Whirligig*. It was almost three hours long – an obscene length for a cartoon – and set in a fairground in Pontefract. The narrative was propelled by the antics of a thin, shiny, creepy man, the owner of the swing ride, and his mischievous daughters who tricked him into making the swings go round too fast. It had a gothic sensibility – stormy skies and abandoned suburbs and uncanny, repetitious motifs. The storyline was periodically interrupted by documentary footage of real people on real-life chair swings at the fair. Their faces went hurtling past the camera, the skin of their knuckles stretched pale and thin where their hands gripped the chains. While she was watching the film, I would slip off to sketch. One afternoon, she stopped me to make an observation.

'I know this is your favourite part,' she said.

'What part?' I said.

She paused the tape. On screen, the two mischievous daughters were about to pull a large metal lever to make the swings go faster still.

'The part where you go back to your work.'

'Would you like me to stay?' I asked.

'No,' she said coolly, eyes still on the television. 'I just wanted you to know that I know. That I know you very well.' She wrapped the blanket more snugly around her. She seemed very pleased with herself. I wondered how much of myself I ought to have abandoned in order to be a good mother to her. I wondered if I was truly within my rights to do anything at all.

Fourteen

She became chronically late. She wasn't lazy and she wasn't tired, but she was never on time. Like the shaking, I thought, it was part of some cryptic pathology. To get her on the school bus, I coached her out of bed. I put breakfast in front of her, hot coffee, buttered toast. She never ate because, no matter when I woke her, there was never enough time. I manoeuvred her into the shower, counted the seconds as she brushed her teeth. She did everything slowly, as if her body were too heavy to move. I shoved snacks in her school bag to assuage my guilt that she hadn't eaten anything. I pushed her arms into sweatshirts and blazers. I pulled a comb through her tangle of hair. Though she was often apologetic and embarrassed when she missed things – when she had to ask me to drive her to school – the prospect of lateness seemed to thrill her. It was a subtle act of rebellion, a way of marking herself out. *This life I've been born into,* she seemed to be saying through her wager with time, *it's not what I would have chosen for myself.*

She never belonged to a particular social group. Rather she had a habit of singling people out and developing intense attachments, brief love affairs that would usually end in disappointment. *I have a new friend,* she would announce every couple of months, and for a few weeks that friend was all she could talk about: the lunches they brought to school, the brand of shoes they wore, what they wanted to be when they grew up. Her experiments with eyeliner, hair dye – the blunt fringe she cut herself with the kitchen scissors – were always influenced by this person. She could look prim and neat like a prefect, or she could look dirty and untamed. The transformations were swift and disarming. I became accustomed to finding her strange.

Often, her new friends took advantage of her. They wanted to copy her homework but would later renege on their weekend plans; they borrowed her CDs, but didn't bother to invite her to the party where they would be played. Once, she loaned a sweater to a friend that was never returned. It was one of my favourites, a beautiful forest green. When she asked her friend about it, the friend claimed to have given it back. She said that my daughter must have lost it and forgotten, perhaps left it on the bus after school. A year or so later, the same girl came to our house to work on an art project at the weekend. My daughter liked to host her schoolmates for these kinds of things. She would tell them that her mother was a *real artist*, with *real canvases, real paints.* When the girl arrived, she was wearing the jumper, by then a little too small, the vibrant green somewhat dulled.

'I like your jumper,' I told her, then turning to my daughter: 'Didn't you used to have one just like that?'

The girl realised her mistake immediately. Her face flushed red. My daughter looked at me, and then the girl.

'No,' she said. 'I don't think so.'

The girl sighed and appeared to relax.

'I had one similar, maybe,' my daughter went on. 'But I never liked it. It was ugly, it didn't suit me. It wouldn't suit anyone, really. I threw it away. Who'd want a jumper like that?'

As she spoke, the girl seemed to shrink, to shrivel in her chair. In being wronged, my daughter was powerful. She took up the moral high ground, wielding it like a weapon.

Fifteen

Towards the end of high school, the head teacher called me in for a meeting. There had been *an incident*. She had missed too many classes, I thought. She had been late too many times. I arrived at his office and his secretary asked me to wait. I sat on an ugly striped sofa with vandalised wooden arms. I stared at an awful picture of a bird taking flight on a beach, presumably painted by one of the students. It was oddly proportioned: two thirds of the picture was sand and shale, rendered in thick brown lines. The clouds in the truncated upper portion of the painting were heavy and opaque. The sky itself had a purplish tinge. On the plastic frame, in claggy orange letters, the student had painted the words: *the sky is the limit.*

There were no windows in the head teacher's office. Mounted on the wall behind him were various certificates and a whole-school photograph. I searched for my daughter's face but couldn't find it. The head teacher was a squat man. His jacket was too small. His large face was grey and dry-looking, his lips the same pale colour as his skin. He told me that he learned of a *squabble* between *some of the ladies* in lower sixth.

'I'm sure your daughter has mentioned it to you,' he said.

I nodded, though she had mentioned nothing, and then I told him that, for the sake of clarity, I'd like to hear what he knew.

He pulled several crumpled sheets of A4 paper from a drawer in his desk and slid them towards me. I felt his eyes on me. He'd been looking forward to this, I realised. This was his big reveal.

At first glance, they looked like posters – the kind a child might make on a word processor to advertise a bake sale or a church fete. I looked more closely and I saw that, at the centre of each of them, was a photo of my daughter. There she was, eating a sandwich from her lunch box on a picnic bench. There she was, lifting her gym bag from a high locker in the changing rooms. She was lacing her shoes at the bus stop. She was opening the door of the girls' toilets. Laid over these images, in lurid word art, were insults like *mutant*, *abortion*, *virus*, and computer instructions: *cancel, delete, eject*. I felt something resolve in my body, the way I had felt when she cried as a baby – blood shifting, bones hardening and becoming more sure of themselves.

'What are these?' I asked. 'Who made them?'

The head teacher raised an eyebrow. One side of his mouth curled up. My ignorance delighted him.

I examined the photographs. They had been taken surreptitiously. They were unposed, intimate, unflattering, somehow ridiculous – her everyday actions rendered absurd. Her skin looked uneven and grey. Her clothes appeared dirty and crumpled. Captured this way, her life took on the pallor of the lives most often displayed in CCTV footage: criminals, missing persons, people up to no good.

'What are you going to do?' I asked.

He said that he'd spoken with my daughter and that she didn't want the other girls to be punished. She was *taking the high road*, he said. It was commendable. I had raised a strong, resilient child.

I considered this – if my daughter really had forgiven them, or if she had her own punishments in mind. 'So you're not doing anything,' I said.

'On the contrary,' he said. 'I've done precisely what the situation requires.'

He said he had *taken the trouble of telling the ladies involved what he thought*. He had encouraged my daughter to make use of the school's *robust suite of welfare provisions*. She would be offered counselling; she could use the meditation room. She had been placed in a different group for her French class, so that she wouldn't have to see the offending girls anymore. She would be given an extra session with the careers adviser.

'She was in the top set for French,' I said.

'Her grades won't be affected,' he replied.

'What does careers advice have to do with anything?'

'It's good for young people to focus on the future,' he replied. 'Not to get stuck in the past.'

I asked him what would happen if I didn't want her to take the high road, if I thought that cruelty ought to be punished.

He suggested that I should think carefully about undermining her wishes, her autonomy. She had expressed her thoughts on the matter and, regardless of what *her mother* felt about the situation, he believed them to be worthy of our respect. Parents, he said, were often hasty when it came to matters like this. Mothers, in particular, could be *overanxious, easily spooked.*

Over the next few days, I watched her carefully. She did not seem troubled. If anything, she was more confident than she had ever been. She went to bed early. She ate large meals. Every night, she read for an hour. When I asked her about the posters, she was a little surprised but still composed.

'I don't know why those girls are so interested in me,' she said.

'You're not upset?'

She was quiet for moment, thinking. 'You're right,' she said. 'I was upset at first.'

'And now?'

She started to pull her ponytail from its elastic band, to run her fingers through her hair. She told me about the girls, when they had joined the school, what they were good at, the challenges and the pressures they faced. 'I think they're sad,' she said. 'They don't know how to let it out.'

'That doesn't make it okay.'

'But I don't mind if they find me interesting,' she said. 'I don't mind if they're a bit obsessed with me.'

'Is this why you never want to go to school?'

'I do want to go to school,' she said. 'I like school.'

'You're always late.'

'That's different,' she said.

'You're not scared?'

She laughed and said, if anything, she was bored.

Sixteen

Before she left for university, I was fearful while she was calm. I thought it would be difficult for her to make friends, or that she would make bad ones as she had in school. I didn't know how her body would respond to the change, if the shaking would return more forcefully and affect her ability to study, to make a new home. I slept poorly and hardly ate, but I recognised my nervous state as something more complex than anxiety or dread. It was cut with excitement because part of my work as a mother was done. We were entering a new phase, one in which I expected great things for myself.

When I asked my daughter how she felt, she only said: 'Fine. It'll be harder on you.'

On moving day, we battled with three suitcases, the double-layered thermal duvet, the endless blankets I'd bought for her. We dragged them through a crowded university car park and up three flights of stairs. When we arrived at her room, there was music playing next door, something burning in the kitchen. I felt ancient. My arms ached. We made two more trips. By the time the car was fully unloaded, we were sweaty and breathless. Neither of us felt like pulling the other into a hug. I wanted to say something significant; when I'd rehearsed this moment, it had felt profound. But she was glancing over my shoulder, watching other people's parents walk by. She put a hand on my shoulder, as though to silence me. I thought she might be the one to speak – to say *thank you for everything*, or *you've given me everything I need* – but she stayed quiet. I kissed her cheek and then her forehead. When I pulled away, her cheeks were red. Her hands were shaking. She turned away to look out of the window and sighed.

'What is it?' I said.

'Don't be emotional.'

'I'm not.'

'You are,' she said.

'Have I embarrassed you?' I asked.

She shook her head.

'What is it?'

'Nothing.'

I waited a moment.

'It's nothing. Let's not drag it out.'

'All right,' I said, but I couldn't help myself: 'What have I done?'

'I don't want to talk about it now.'

'All right. Then when?'

She took a few deep breaths. 'Look,' she said. 'Don't call

me. If you're lonely, I don't want you to be calling me all the time.'

'I'll be fine,' I told her. 'I'm used to being on my own.'

'You're lying,' she said.

I laughed.

Her face hardened. 'Could you just go? Please, just go.'

I waited another moment, then turned and walked back down the hall.

I had been wrong about her – she settled in wonderfully, she made plenty of friends – but she was right about me.

There was a brief period of elation, where I ate sugared cereal for dinner and listened to loud music late at night. I drank whole bottles of wine and had midnight snacks on the living room floor – hazelnut yoghurts, caramel chocolates, peppered crackers, soft cheese. I tried to remember what life had been like before I was a mother. There had been friends. I'd lived in the city. Every other weekend, I'd gone to see my father, and, though I loved him deeply, I was always relieved when the visit was over. Parents like to pretend they know their children, I thought, but really, it's the other way around. Your children will always surprise you while, to them, you're the most predictable thing in the world.

Within a few weeks of her departure, I didn't know when to get out of bed, when to eat, when to get dressed. There were no conversations at the end of the school day, no need to cook for someone else. I spent days in the same pyjamas, I washed my hair infrequently. There was some pleasure, I found, in laziness, but there was also self-disgust. I told myself that it was a phase, that I'd be better by Christmas, when she came home. I tried to give myself a proper routine. I resolved to wake up before eight, to go to the studio every afternoon, to eat three meals a day, to deliver myself back to bed before midnight, but I couldn't make it stick. I became resentful. It seemed unfair that I wasn't more interested in my life, as though it had been falsely advertised. I was angry with myself for not being able to paint anything good, and then I was angry at everything: the news, the weather, the sweeping noise of the cars on the road, world politics, my general health. The rage was exhausting and I started to sleep a little better at night, but when it dissipated, an overwhelming sadness took its place. It was as if I had been proven right. *You were always going to end up like this. You were just fooling yourself until now.* Depression was smug, it was so pleased with itself. *How right you were,* it seemed to say, *to fear that everything was about to go wrong.*

I called my daughter every night. She was my only connection to the outside world. I tried not to cry, but I often did. I tried not to sound weak, but my voice always cracked. She listened to everything I had to say. She let me sob down the phone. She exercised enormous patience, telling me I was loved, that things would improve. Her advice was always practical. *Eat breakfast. Get a hobby. Buy a pet. Leave the house at least once a day.* She told me to see more people, to go out and find friends of my own. I knew, even as I ignored her, that she was right, but I had already convinced myself that none of it was important. So what if I ate properly, if I had interests and healthy routines? I would only be pretending to have a good and wholesome life. That's the real trick of depression. It talks you out of the solution before the attempt.

I forced myself to go to the studio, but none of my efforts were any good. I hated being there. I felt precious and vain. I thought of my father, and how often he'd told me to do what I loved. I thought how much easier things might have been if, instead, I'd done something normal – something with regular hours, with colleagues and discrete tasks, something that didn't require my whole self. I took a long break from painting. It felt like a surrender, as if I were giving myself over to fate. I assumed that, eventually, something would happen to sweep me back to my old life, or to set me on a new course. Instead, circumstances simply continued to accrue until the situation reached a point of no return. I had no money. My only asset was the house. It was impossible to think of selling it – my daughter had lived there all her life – so I put it up for rent. There was nowhere to go in the village, and I had no particular reason to stay, so I returned to Leeds, where I had once been a student, and moved into a one-bed flat.

Seventeen

Living in an apartment suited me. I liked hearing the neighbours above and below. I found myself feeling less depressed, but also less real. I got stuck in the present moment, no longer able to look forward or back. Each new day appeared as if there had never been any others, as if there may never be more. I didn't think about my childhood or my father; I was at a remove from where my daughter had grown. I supposed that I was free to become a new person, but until that person emerged, I was floating, in-between.

When she came to stay with me in the holidays, we stumbled over each other. She would alternate between sharing my bed and trying to sleep on the sofa, silently resenting me for not providing her with her own room. She liked to tell me off me for staying up too late and then again for not getting up in the morning. The more independent she became, the more she learned of adult life, the more she seemed dissatisfied, perhaps even insulted, by the choices I'd made.

'You need to go back to painting,' she told me once, over dinner. 'If you were painting, all this' – she gestured dismissively towards the living area – 'would make some kind of sense.'

'I'm thinking about it,' I lied.

My daughter was now painting a lot. She took extracurricular art classes twice a week. I knew she liked it, but her enthusiasm for it felt spiteful, or at least calculated. It was as if she thought, by telling me how easy it was, I'd suddenly remember how to do it myself.

'You have to do something,' she said. She started sending me information about local groups, evening classes. But I had never understood hobbies. For me, the only way to love something was to turn it into work.

I did not learn pottery or patisserie-making or apiculture, but I did get into the habit of leaving the house. Every morning, I went for a walk. If I couldn't sleep, I got up with the sun and wandered the city while the streets were quiet. I walked until my legs ached, then I bought coffee and walked some more. I got a new sketchbook and started drawing every day. It was a slow and effortful process, like an athlete recovering strength after an injury. I bought a new phone and took pictures of people when they weren't looking, the uglier the posture the better. I caught them mid-sentence, mid-meal. I liked how awkward the images were, how ungainly, unrefined. Then, in painstaking detail, I rendered these images in pencil – uncomposed, oddly proportioned but perfectly done. While I worked, I thought about my daughter, how she'd turned out so well. She was strong and reliable, she had a clear plan for herself. When she graduated with high marks, she got a legal traineeship at a Sheffield firm. I was pleased, and a little relieved, that she had chosen a steady career. I also knew that, had I been more successful, more financially secure, she would have chosen something else.

Eighteen

There must have been boyfriends before Paul, but I never heard about them. When she first told me about him, I had an odd, out-of-body feeling, as if she were recreating a scene from someone else's life. Her language sounded false, unnatural, repurposed from elsewhere. *I've met someone. I've never been so happy. We work together. It's going really well.*

Just as robotically, I told her I was pleased.

She said I could at least pretend to be happy for her.

'If you're happy,' I began—

'Don't give me that,' she said.

I asked when I might meet him.

'He's shy,' she said. 'When you meet him, you have to be kind.'

'I'm always kind,' I said.

'I know that,' she countered. 'But sometimes you have to do it in a way other people can understand.'

Several months passed. I'd ask her how he was, and she'd always answer in terms of work. *He's getting on better with our colleagues. We have a new manager who likes him. He's out tonight because he closed a case.* She measured his confidence in volubility – I was always hearing about how much he'd had to say in meetings, or not, and how this related to his progress overall. It was hard to form a clear impression of a person when all you knew of them was their relations with their fellow office staff. She talked about him as if he were a puppy she were training, noting major milestones and achievements, discussing his behaviour as if she were waiting for it to improve.

'What's he really like?' I asked her once. 'Outside of work.'

'Oh, he's lovely,' she said. 'Sweet.'

'What do you do together?'

She listed a number of unimaginative activities: movies, restaurants, weekend walks in the countryside.

I pictured him like all the terrible men my friends had dated in their twenties – men with complex needs. Together, we would analyse and dissect them, as though the ability to construct a compelling psychological profile were more important than basic things like kindness and humour. I had been working in an office then, too. It had made me monumentally unhappy – not depressed, not bored, but quite incredulous at how ill-suited I was to having my time managed by anyone else. Kind men were attracted to my misery. It was interesting to them. They considered it an aesthetic position, a studied demeanour that came across as aloof and superior, when in fact I felt worthless and dull. My friends were stylish and well adjusted, far more beautiful than me. Somehow, they ended up with strange and protean men who required delicate handling and emotional care. Perversely, all the good men came to me and I could not love them, so I avoided relationships altogether. Even after I learned I was pregnant, I never told my daughter's father, though he was kind and patient and perhaps would have cared for us. I didn't tell my friends either because, after my father died, it was as if too much had changed for me to go back to my old life. I couldn't explain myself to them. So, my daughter had grown up without community, without knowing any men, and it seemed probable that, like my friends, she would choose poorly for herself.

Eventually, I did meet Paul. He was of average height, slim build, with a sallow complexion. His hair was mousy, greasy-looking. He had a downturned mouth. In certain lights, there were some pleasing angles to his face, but when he wasn't concentrating, when his features weren't arranged in a particular expression, he appeared ugly and withdrawn. He wore the kind of oversized cardigans my father used to wear; his glasses were too big for his face. He had chameleon-like abilities that I found unsettling to observe. His general demeanour could change quickly. He might be warm and loquacious at one moment and then choose to disappear the next.

The first time I met him, she brought him to Leeds. We went to an Italian restaurant, Umberto's, where the music was loud and farcical, 'Nessun Dorma' and 'That's Amore'. The decor was low-budget period film: papier mâché sculptures, cardboard columns in the Doric style, green vines and exuberant bunches of plastic grapes. I liked it there because the pasta was fresh and because it had none of the artfulness of fine dining. There were breadsticks and bread baskets served with plastic tubs of butter. There were polyester flowers on the table beside large glass bowls of parmesan cheese. At the end of the meal, filter coffee was served from a jug with a complimentary liqueur, limoncello or Frangelico.

As we were shown to our table, Paul, who had previously been shy as she'd described, shifted gear and became loud. He made a joke about the music. He sang a line from a song he knew. When the waiter brought us the menus, he said *grazie, amico,* and even my daughter seemed surprised at that. This jocular performance lasted all through the meal. I thought perhaps it was the wine but, as I walked with them back to the station, he withdrew. His face turned blank. My daughter spoke to him and he didn't respond. He walked a few paces ahead of us, leaving us to talk between ourselves.

'Is he all right?' I asked her.

She looked at me, surprised. 'Why wouldn't he be?'

'He's very quiet.'

'You're quiet sometimes, too,' she said.

'Not like that.'

She rolled her eyes. 'I knew you'd have something bad to say.'

I started to defend myself.

'I know, I know. If I'm happy,' she said. 'That's all that

matters to you.' She changed the subject. She talked briefly about work. She wanted to know what I'd been doing lately and I made up a few things.

'I won't ask if you're painting,' she said.

When I got back to the flat, I was restless. I hadn't done what I set out to do: I hadn't told her what I really thought or warned her about what men like him could become. I tried to reason with myself. I didn't really know him; perhaps he wasn't so bad. He might not make a good first impression, or he might be someone I could grow to like. But I felt I was right about him. He was sinister, mercurial. He would not be kind to her – I couldn't rationalise it, but I was sure.

Later that night, she sent a text message, apologising. I was free to think what I liked, she said. She wanted to thank me for *being nice*. Paul enjoyed the food, she said. He had a pleasant time. I realised, then, my mistake: I had thought she was disappointed in me, that she'd wanted me to like him, when in fact her primary concern was what he might think of me. She had expected me to embarrass her, but I had not. She was letting me know that my behaviour was passable, and now she was relieved.

Nineteen

I hoped that Paul would be a transitional object, something she could hold onto while she built her adult life, and that, once this life was fully formed, she'd let him go. But after I'd met him a few times, it occurred to me that I was used to him. This disturbed me. It was strange to have put so much time into a person I had not chosen for myself.

They moved in together. With money from his parents, Paul bought a Victorian mid-terrace in a suburb populated by artisanal cheese shops and cafés with bare concrete walls. My daughter paid him rent. It was a nice area, she told me. There was a bakery, a farmers' market on Saturdays. She never invited me over to their house. She always said that they were *doing it up*, as though they lived in a continual state of improvement. On the phone, she talked about their *current projects*: a piece of furniture they were restoring, the beautiful colour they had painted the hallway. While she described in detail these devotional acts, I found myself thinking of the old stone house where we never renovated or restored or repainted, where things crumbled and deteriorated in our midst. I had found it freeing not to care – I didn't need my kitchen or my living room to communicate anything in particular about me – but I wondered, then, if she'd hated our house, and whether or not she'd felt ashamed.

For a couple of years, I didn't see her very much. We talked often enough, but she was always busy with her work. If I suggested we meet, there was always something more pressing she had to do. I became used to her excuses, they didn't upset me anymore. I kept inviting her, I knew she still worried about me and that eventually she would feel obliged to come. Meanwhile, I recovered a sense of optimism. For the first time, she didn't need me and nor did I particularly need her. I was filled with a spacious feeling, not freedom exactly, but a sense of possibility. I started working again. I rented studio space in an old mill near the university. My canvases were larger than before – too large to go above anyone's sofas, and too ugly, I thought, for anyone buy.

I was still working from photographs – the awkward shots of unsuspecting subjects, badly lit, in unflattering postures. One image, taken on a slant, showed a haphazard line of empty wooden chairs in a cafeteria. At the edge of the frame was a woman's skirt and leg. Another showed a man eating a supermarket sandwich while waiting for a bus and the blurred arm of a woman who stepped out in front of me just as the camera clicked. They were the kinds of pictures you took accidentally and later deleted, but I made them huge. I rendered them in oils, as realistically as I could. I had started to enjoy my own company once more. When we finally saw one another, I would tell her about it, I thought. She would see all the progress I had made. I would have something to say for myself.

Just before her birthday, she announced that she was coming to visit. I offered to cook for her at the flat. It was late May. The evenings were getting lighter and I'd been spending long hours at the studio. If the weather was fine, I thought, I would take her to see what I'd done. All afternoon, I cooked and cleaned. I wanted her to see how my life had improved. I arranged fresh flowers on the table. I bought her favourite chocolates. I bought her a hand-painted silk scarf in her favourite shades of green. Then the text messages started to arrive. At first, she said she was running late. I told her to take her time, not to rush. At seven o'clock, she said she still hadn't managed to get on a train. She was at home. She just needed to change. Then she went quiet. An hour later, a strange message appeared. It didn't sound like her. *It's not happening tonight*, the message began. *Work has got the better of me.* I'd never heard her use that phrase before. My daughter was smart, hard-working, she knew the value of her own skills. I didn't believe she thought her work had ever *got the better of her*; it was only her body that had done that. I felt sure that the message wasn't really from her.

I considered how best to respond. If she wasn't the one holding the phone, I didn't want to do anything that might make her situation worse. *I'm so sorry,* I wrote. *You must be very tired. Perhaps we could talk on the phone instead?*

I don't want to talk right now, came the reply, followed by a separate message with an *x*. She never usually sent anything with a kiss.

All evening, I felt very unwell. I wanted to go to her. I knew something was wrong, but if I overreacted, she would be humiliated, angry. The risks were impossible to calculate, I had too little information. A wrong move could push her further away. I thought: this is what it means to have a grown-up child – the same desperate need to care for them, but all the power gone.

Twenty

The next day, her messages were normal again. She apologised, said that she missed me and that we'd see each other soon, but it didn't happen for several weeks. Every couple of days, she'd suggest a new date, then something would come up and she'd cancel again. I remained amenable, understanding. *Just whenever you're free*, I wrote. *I'll be so glad to see you.* She was never free, it seemed. I continued to work on the paintings. I immersed myself in them. I didn't think about composition – I wanted them to feel artless, as the photographs did – but the details of the images were complicated and required careful attention. Subjects stood in front of one another and blocked each other's light; something was moving in the background, becoming blurry and indistinct. It wasn't possible to see the whole as it emerged. I was forced to focus on the particulars, one at a time.

*

One day, out of the blue, she called to ask if I was busy and then she said she would get the ten thirty train.

'Don't you have to work?' I asked. It was early on a Tuesday.

'You never used to work in the mornings,' she said vaguely. 'I never really knew what you did with that time.'

'Housework, mostly. Or the shopping.'

'The house was always such a mess,' she said. Her voice was quiet and faraway. It didn't sound like an accusation, it sounded more like nostalgia.

I went to meet her at the station. I wrapped my arms around her and held her close for a long time.

The first thing she said was: 'You don't look so good.'

'Thanks,' I said.

'Are you ill?'

'No.'

'You're sure?'

'I'm working again,' I told her. 'Big canvases. I work on the floor.'

She raised an eyebrow, then looked away. 'You might be too old for that,' she said.

I had been looking forward to telling her about it; I hoped she'd be glad, even proud. I thought of the times she brought her school friends back to the stone house, how she had shown them the materials of her artist mother's life: exhibition posters, prints, abandoned canvases. But she wasn't interested. She appeared preoccupied, looking nervously about her as though she was expecting someone to arrive.

'You don't look quite yourself either,' I told her. She was

pale. There was a patch of dry skin beneath one eye. Her clothes seemed shapeless on her body, as if they belonged to someone else.

'I've been ill,' she said.

'Oh?' She hadn't mentioned anything on the phone.

'I'm tired all the time,' she said. 'I don't feel like I've got any strength.'

'Are you in pain?'

'Not yet,' she said, and yawned.

I asked her if she'd been to the doctor. She said she didn't think it would help. This was a hangover from her childhood of failed appointments and ineffectual therapies. She had no faith in medical professionals anymore. She never expected anyone else to understand her body. She saw her health, her general well-being, as something that only she could control.

It started to rain and so I took her to a nearby cafeteria, an old-fashioned place with red and white tiles on the floor. We sat at a table by the window. My daughter was distracted, elsewhere. It took her a long time to take off her coat, as though she couldn't remember how to coordinate the movement of her arms. She gazed outside, fixing her eyes on passers-by, craning to follow them until they turned out of sight.

'Are you worried about something?' I said.

'No,' she said.

'How's work?'

'He's fine.'

'I said, "how's work"?'

'Oh, that's fine too.' Her hands were folded softly in her lap, no trembling. Her lips were drawn tight.

'Are you hungry?'

'I'm not sure,' she said. She sighed and rested against the window, pressing her forehead to the glass.

At that moment, a man went by – average height, mousy hair. He was walking at pace, carrying a briefcase, which clipped the window as he passed. It spilled open, sending its contents across the pavement: some papers, a lunch box, a tie, a gleaming watch. Panicked, the man got down on his knees and groped for the papers, which were already muddied and damp. With frantic motions, he flung his possessions back into the briefcase and slammed it shut, but righting himself too quickly, he tripped and fell.

In slow motion, I saw his body tip towards us. The briefcase fell to the floor once again. I watched the movement of his hair in the breeze, the ugly expression shifting in his eyes. He put out his hands to break the fall, slapping the glass of the cafeteria window right by our faces. The bones of his knuckles showed translucent-white through the skin of his palm, surrounded by small red lines. There were fat blue veins in his wrist, dark hairs sprouting up the arm, an oval-shaped mole at the base of the thumb. A long second passed where I looked at him and he looked at me – two people who were nothing to do with one another. I slid my chair away, disorientated by the feeling that something had been about to hit us, all while knowing that this was impossible, that the glass was in the way.

The sound of the dry slap of the man's hands against the

window reverberated for a moment. With effort, he stood up. His face was red and purple, the colour of organs in anatomical diagrams, the chambers of the heart or the dark substance of the liver. He composed himself, walked on and quickly vanished in the jumble of bodies near the station. When I looked over at my daughter, she had her head down on the table. She had covered her ears with her hands. She was shaking violently.

I reached out to touch her and she flinched. She made a small, high-pitched noise.

'It's all right,' I said. 'He's gone.'

She moved her head from side to side. Her shoulders trembled. 'No,' she said. 'No, no.'

'What is it?' I asked. I reached out to touch her and she withdrew.

As she sat up, her eyes were heavy. She didn't seem to know what to do with her hands. She kept moving them from her cheeks to the base of her neck to the table and back again. The flesh of her arms was pimpled and taut. A waiter came over to take our order. He asked if we were all right. I looked at her and waited for her to speak. She said that she didn't care what we ate, that she would just have the same as me, and when it arrived she only picked at her food. She extracted two thick slices of ham from her sandwich and proceeded to cut them into bite-size squares. Then she pulled out the slivers of gherkin with her fingers and ate them slowly, one by one. By the time I'd eaten my whole sandwich, a salad garnish and a handful of crisps, her plate was still full.

'You don't like it?' I asked.

She looked blank. Her eyes shone.

'What's happened to you?' I said. The question came as a relief. When she was small and could not stop shaking, I had thought this over and over – *Who are you? What's happening to you?* – but she had been too young to ask.

Her lips parted. I watched her. I waited for her to speak, observing her tensed mouth, a small black shape.

'Has he done something to you?' I said.

Her right hand trembled the knife she had been using to cut the ham. Then, as if she had only just heard the words, she said: 'What do you mean?'

I held her gaze. She looked away. The lines of her face were sadder, somehow. I had a vision of their life together, hers and Paul's, that was hateful and dark. 'He hurt you,' I said gently.

'Are you asking me or telling me?'

'It's what I think. He hurt you.'

'He never hit me,' she said.

'Okay,' I said. 'That's not the only way to hurt someone.' I remembered the girls from school, how she had dismissed their cruelty, the head teacher who had called her *resilient*. A real sadist, I thought, would take great pleasure in testing her, in finding the edges of what my daughter would endure.

'You can tell me,' I told her. 'I love you.'

Something snapped. 'No,' she said. 'Stop making things up. You never liked him. You never like anyone. But not everyone hates men like you do.' Then she laughed, as if nothing was serious, as if our whole conversation were light-hearted, a game.

She finished her sandwich quickly, then. The rain had stopped, and the street gleamed beneath the sun. I looked for evidence of the man who had fallen – some mark on the glass where his hands had been, some abandoned paperwork – but saw nothing.

'Shall we go for a walk?' she asked.

Twenty-One

When the mother of the missing son wrote to me, she was grieving a betrayal. Her son was no longer loyal to her; he appeared to have forgotten all she had done. She wanted me to explain his behaviour, to understand how my daughter had brought about the change. I wanted to tell her there were no real ties: her son was, as he had always been, entirely free. For me, the ache of motherhood has been to know that my daughter owes me nothing, that I deserve nothing, while at the same time wanting so much from her. A good mother would be able to contain this wanting; perhaps that's all good mothering is. As we left the café that day and walked in the direction of the studio, the sky remained overcast, but sun spilled down between the clouds, warm and hopeful on our backs. The streets were quieter and she appeared to relax. She looked more like herself, or she looked more like my idea of who she was. I had the feeling that something special was about to take place between us. I would show her my paintings, and that – even though they were loose and unfinished, and it was unclear what they might yet become – she would find them interesting. The whole experience, I thought, would facilitate a closeness, a renewed bond between mother and daughter, that she would know I was well in myself and therefore could feel free to confide in me.

I hadn't told her where we were going. When we came upon the studio, I asked her if she would like to see my new work. She looked surprised. She narrowed her eyes.

'Is it finished?' she asked.

'No.'

'Are you sure you want to be showing it to people, then?'

'You're not people,' I said. 'You're my daughter.'

She shrugged.

I unlocked the door. I led her through the breeze-blocked corridor, up the difficult, steep staircase and into the work-space. It was cold and dark. There were two large paintings on the floor – giant canvases I had to walk around and climb upon – that it was difficult to see the entirety of at any one time.

'I've been working from photographs again,' I said.

My daughter said nothing. She stayed where she was, by the door.

'I don't know how many paintings there will be,' I went on. 'But I haven't worked like this for a long time.'

I wanted her to acknowledge my breakthrough, to feel

the thrill of it with me. 'That's nice,' she said, carefully. She looked around, observing the cracked plasterwork on the walls, the heap of rubbish in the corner left by the studio's previous resident. Then slowly she walked towards a trestle table where the photographs were laid. One by one, she held the prints, examining them closely.

'This might be illegal,' she said. 'Did you take these on private land?'

'What? No.'

'If someone could identify themselves, and remembered where you were—'

'I wasn't asking for your professional opinion,' I said. 'No one's identifiable. That's the point.'

'So the point is to paint someone but not make them truly themselves?'

'That's not what I said.'

'So you do want them to be themselves, but not to know that you've painted them?'

'They're throwaway images. They're not proper photographs. I wouldn't care if someone photographed half my leg and then painted it. I wouldn't ever need to know.'

'You'd know,' she said. 'You'd feel it.' She dropped the photographs onto the table and turned to the canvases themselves, stalking around them with an expression of disgust.

'I'm sorry you don't like them,' I said. She could see that I was upset.

'I don't like them,' she confirmed.

'I thought you'd be pleased. You wanted me to work.'

She looked at me and I felt small, foolish. 'I don't want to be here anymore,' she said.

We walked back towards the station at pace. A light rain was falling again, dull and flat with no sun to reflect. A group of students pushed past us, among them a young woman crying, helped along by several friends. My daughter stopped to watch them. She seemed concerned, unsettled. Her body was restless in a way that was familiar to me. I tried placing a hand on her arm. Again, she pulled away. I was panicked. I wanted to tell her again that I loved her, but I knew it wouldn't help. Instead, at the station entrance, I asked her to stay.

She fumbled in her bag for her ticket, found it, put it back in her purse, took it out again.

'Don't go,' I implored. 'Call in sick tomorrow. Have a rest.'

She was bouncing a little on her toes, looking over one shoulder then the other.

'Will Paul make dinner tonight?' I asked. 'You could call him to say you won't be back. Would he understand? If you weren't there?'

'He wouldn't like it,' she said.

'Is he angry a lot?' I asked.

'I never said he was angry.'

'What, then?'

She hesitated. She wanted to tell me, I thought, and perhaps she would have if I had stayed quiet, but I couldn't help it.

'Why didn't you like the paintings?' I said.

She looked at me and backed away in the direction of the platform, ticket in hand.

I followed closely. 'I'm sorry,' I said.

She told me to leave her alone.

'You can stay with me,' I told her. 'I can look after you.'

She walked faster, putting distance between us, then she turned and said loudly: 'You only care about yourself.'

Twenty-Two

I didn't hear from her that evening. She didn't reply to any of my messages asking if she was home safely, or if her train had been delayed on account of the storm. The next day, I rang her office, pretending to be somebody else. Her assistant told me she was in meetings all morning, and the moment of relief – she was okay, she'd gone to work – was quickly countered by frustration. I wanted to ask: how is she? Does she look well-rested? Did she arrive with Paul? Is he kind to her at work? I thanked the assistant, hung up and cried.

Several weeks passed. Every day, I tried to reach her. When her silence became too much, I called her assistant again. This time, she wasn't in meetings – her assistant said she was free to talk. I was taken aback. I'd assumed she took calls by appointment, and I hadn't prepared what to say.

'It's your mother,' I said.

'What do you want?'

'I was worried.'

'Well, don't be.'

'I can't help it.'

'But what good does it do?' she said.

I heard other voices in the background, my daughter saying she'd be right there.

'Work is difficult at the moment,' she said quietly. 'Not everyone thinks I'm doing a good job.'

'You've always done a good job,' I told her. 'You've always done so well.'

Her voice brightened. 'Thank you,' she said.

I said it again. I told her that was what I really thought.

'I'll call you later,' she said warmly.

A few days later, she did call.

There followed a brief period where we talked a lot. I apologised for all kinds of things. She allowed me to speak but offered little by way of response. I asked her about work, who it was that was giving her a hard time, and she said nothing. I asked about Paul and she avoided this too. Instead, she remembered things from her childhood: birthday festivities from two decades earlier, bonfire nights with huge open fires in the garden, the old bed sheets we had painted in vibrant colours and hung from the tree to dry. Her memories were often attached to the garden, to particular seasons and the senses they awakened: the stale damp earth of autumn, the fresh hope of spring. Broadly, our memories aligned but there were sometimes discrepancies in the details. I remembered the bonfire being large and wild, for example, while she said it was tame. I thought it had been her idea to paint the sheets, but she assured me it was mine. *Everything was your idea back then*, she said. *I was just a child.* I indulged her recollections. I gave up trying to steer the conversation too much. If I could make my words light enough, if I could meet her very gently, it seemed possible that our relationship could repair.

Then she stopped answering my calls. *Things are bad at work,* she wrote in her text messages. *Paul is having a difficult time. Paul really needs me to take care of him.* I asked what I could do to help. Did she want to come and stay? Could I visit her? I wished I still lived in the old stone house, feeling sure that, if I did, she would have come home. My propositions became wilder and more desperate. We could go travelling. She could take a sabbatical from work. Suddenly, it occurred to me that there were so many things we'd never done. We'd never really had a holiday, except for the occasional weekend by the sea, or an overnight stay in a hotel before an exhibition. Had we ever been to the theatre? Had I ever taken her to the zoo? What did normal mothers do with their grown-up daughters? I imagined shopping trips and long chatty lunches, or excursions to the countryside: wild swimming, hikes in the rain. We didn't do any of those things. Eventually she wrote to me saying that she didn't want anything, if she wanted something she'd ask for it, and if I truly wished to be helpful then I should leave her alone.

I continued to paint the giant, ugly oil paintings, though I had no expectations of them. I worked long hours, hardly thinking about what I was doing, allowing my body to move mechanically around the task. Months passed and the paintings multiplied, until I started to run out of space. I found it liberating to abandon notions of beauty and concept; I was free to make work that was sprawling and graceless. I knew there was something unsettling about the canvases as they emerged, and that too was pleasing, though I tried not to think of it too much. All that was required of me, in the short term, was to concentrate on a tiny part of each photograph at a time, to render it as faithfully as possible: the colour, the texture, the light.

Beneath the weight of this concentration, memories of my own childhood surfaced. I thought a lot about my father and how he had behaved after my mother had left. The women in the neighbourhood had all pitied him – it was so unnatural for a mother to leave. People told him what terrible luck he'd had, as if he'd had no part to play, as if he'd simply picked some bad fruit – fine on the outside but rotten within. I'd never asked him outright: why do you think she left? I assumed that, like me, he blamed himself.

Twenty-Three

One morning, while working in the studio, I received a call from an unknown number. I was painting a difficult corner, the blurred motion of a dark-coloured coat.

The voice on the other end of the line asked who I was, so I told them.

'Is this a good time?' they said.

'What for?'

'I'm afraid I have some bad news,' the voice explained.

My mind reached for my daughter. Something had happened. He had hurt her, or worse. She had fled and was missing. She had hurt herself. She had hurt him and then herself. It was too late. I hadn't done anything to help her. She had not come to me. I hated Paul. I hated the fact that we no longer lived safely in the old stone house. I thought of all the bloody and heinous crimes I had known men to commit against women. I felt very small and very empty. I looked up at a giant canvas, the first I'd completed in years. It loomed over me and I felt sick.

'What's happened to her?' I said. 'Will she be all right?'

But it wasn't my daughter. My mother had died.

Twenty-Four

I called my daughter and prayed she would answer. I had to tell someone. There was no one else. I waited for the line to connect but her phone was off. I left a voicemail, two voicemails, and then I sent a text. *This is actually important.* She didn't reply. The message remained unread. I walked the long way home. It was spring, before the clocks went forward. There had been a lot of rain and the air smelled green. A change of season always makes me nostalgic. Springtime arrives and I find myself remembering the previous spring, and all the springs before that, and the kinds of things that a spring makes possible. Somehow, a new season always comes as a surprise, as though, by the time the weather shifts, I've come to expect it to be winter forever. My father loved the spring, too, when his garden needed him most. And when my daughter was small, I took her out for bright walks in the pushchair and spent long hours playing with her beneath the tree. Now spring was here and my mother was dead.

I tried my daughter's phone again and again, but it didn't ring. Afternoon became evening. From the sofa, I watched the sky darken and waited for my daughter to call me back. I wondered if my mother had ever thought about calling me, if she had sat by the phone ready to dial. Had she remembered my birthdays? Had she looked me up? Had she seen my work? I realised I knew nothing of her own childhood; she had robbed me of that information, too. Perhaps something terrible had happened when she was younger, so terrible that she found she was unable to be with me. Perhaps it was only when she became a mother herself that she had understood how terrible it really was.

At midnight, when I still hadn't heard from my daughter, I considered my options. I could call her office in the morning. I could drive to Sheffield and wait for her there. Then I remembered that once, when her phone had broken, she had used Paul's to let me know. I scrolled through my call history and found the unsaved number. I sent a message. *It's Bella*, I wrote. *Where is she? I need to talk to her.* I waited a moment, then in another message I added: *My mother has died.*

I lay down on the sofa and closed my eyes. In the space between sleeping and waking, strange scenes emerged. I dreamed that my daughter had also died, that she was with my mother and father in that other place and that, together, they were watching me and laughing.

Twenty-Five

Paul didn't respond until the following morning. *Why are you asking me?* he wrote.

Where is she? I repeated. *Why isn't she answering her phone?*

A few minutes later, he called me. 'She left me,' he said, brusquely.

I said nothing.

'She didn't tell you,' he said.

'No.'

'She doesn't live here anymore.'

'When?' I asked him.

'September,' he said. 'The twenty-third, to be precise.'

Almost six months had passed. 'Where is she now?' I asked him.

'She moved in with a friend from work,' he said.

'Someone nice?'

He paused. 'Yes,' he said. 'She's nice. I can pass on your message.' He sounded weary.

'Thank you,' I said. 'Please. She's not answering her phone,' I explained.

'That sounds like her,' he said. Then he told me that he had an early meeting and hung up.

I thought about going to the studio, but didn't. The paintings had been going well, I didn't want to make a mistake. It was important to keep them safe, so that when I was ready they would still be there for me. Instead, I found an old journal and started to write. I wrote a list of questions, equally applicable to both my mother and my daughter. *Where did you go? Why didn't you explain? What happened to you?* I didn't understand how they could feel so free, without any obligation to tell me the truth. As a mother, I agonised over every mistake. And as a daughter, at fifty-eight years old, I still didn't feel free of my own parents, even now they were both dead.

Twenty-Six

'Are you sure?' my daughter asked when, at last, she called me back.

'Of course I'm sure,' I said. 'Why would I be unsure of something like that?'

There were clinking noises in the background, a cork being pulled from a bottle of wine.

'Where are you?' I pictured her with Paul. I saw him opening the wine smugly, pouring her a glass.

'I'm with a friend,' she said. 'Hang on.' The line became muffled. I heard her say something authoritative, *not now*, or *not here*. Then she was back, talking to me as if we were trying to arrange some matter of business. 'So what will we do? About Grandma?' she said.

'She's not your grandma,' I corrected.

'But she is your mother.'

'Yes,' I said.

'Well then.'

'She can be your *grandmother*, but she isn't just *Grandma*.'

'You haven't answered my question,' she said. 'I assume there are things to do.'

'There's a funeral.'

'You want to go?'

'Not want.'

'But you'll go?'

'Yes, I'll go,' I said.

'Right,' she said and, after she had thought for a moment, she added: 'Why is that?'

'She was my mother.'

'But you didn't know her.'

'I knew her for seven years.'

'You weren't in touch. She didn't know you were an artist, or that you had a daughter.' She said these things as if talking about something she'd heard on the radio, something that interested her vaguely but ultimately had nothing to do with her life.

'She might have known,' I said. 'There were people she might have asked.'

My daughter laughed.

I felt pathetic. 'I don't want to regret not having gone,' I said.

'And you want me to come too.'

I wanted her to say that she would come because she couldn't bear to think of me going alone. I wanted her to understand, without explanation. 'Yes,' I said.

'Fine,' she said, casually. 'But you're not forgiven.'

'For what?' I didn't know which thread of the past she would pull at.

'You know exactly what he's like,' she said. 'And still you called him.'

Twenty-Seven

When she arrived at the door the next day, she hardly looked like my daughter at all. She was much larger than she had been before, much wider in the thighs and the chest. Her skin was bright and clear, her hair gleamed. Her eyes glistened like an animal's eyes. The muscle in her shoulders pushed against the seams of her shirt. She had brought with her an enormous suitcase, bashed up and gaping at one corner.

'You look different,' I said, stupidly. I kissed her face several times and she let me. I drew her towards me and hugged her. She was very warm.

She opened the fridge and poured the remainder of a carton of juice into a glass.

'Are you—'

'I'm great,' she said.

'And you and Paul—'

'Over,' she said. 'And I've quit my job.'

'Because of Paul?'

'Because I've got more important things to do with my time.'

'Why didn't you tell me?' I said.

She manoeuvred the suitcase around the sofa. The zip slipped open and some small objects – among them a tea strainer, bath salts, a small bag of dried herbs – fell to the floor.

'Are you going somewhere?' I said, gesturing towards the suitcase.

'I thought I'd stay here.'

'Here in the flat?' I looked around, at the small bedroom, the kitchen with the sofa and the television in it, the bursting cupboard in the hall.

'You're at the studio all day anyway,' she said.

'In the afternoons.'

'Then I'll work in the mornings,' she said.

'I thought you'd quit your job.'

'Not that kind of work. Is there a gym near here?' she said.

'Did you get a new job?'

She looked at me very calmly. She told me to think of my giant canvases and the ugly people I had painted without their permission. 'It's the opposite of that,' she said.

Twenty-Eight

I tried to prepare myself for the funeral. I thought about how the other mourners might respond when I told them that it was my mother who had died. I rehearsed how I myself would answer to being the daughter of someone I didn't know. But, of course, when we got there, nobody knew who I was and, therefore, nobody asked.

We sat at the back. My daughter took up so much space on the bench that her arm was forced to press against mine. It wasn't affectionate, though it comforted me. After a while she moved away and I felt worse than before. She gulped noisily at a protein drink she had brought in a huge plastic flask. A few people turned to look. The service went on for a long time. My mother's friends got up to speak and I received a great deal of information I had not been prepared to learn.

She had retired at the age of sixty-six having *retrained as a nurse* in middle age. For the last ten years of her life, she had lived in a bungalow with her *dear friend, Agnes*. She loved board games, dessert wines, the crossword, *hamsters*, old musicals, spaghetti, pétanque. She was always threatening to take up tap-dancing. She made *a mean damson cobbler*. She was a sometime *patron of the arts*. Towards the end of the service, dear Agnes herself said a few words. She wore a long black cotton gown with a vibrant pink jacket over the top and lime-green plastic earrings. Her face looked like a crumpled sheet of fabric, draping in folds and tucks so that the expression was hard to read.

'While she was in hospital,' Agnes said, 'people sent her flowers and fruit. Peaches were her favourite. When I couldn't visit, she arranged for a young man to deliver things to me. For three months, I ate peaches and cream. I prayed for her recovery. In her most difficult hour, that was how she was.

She thought a lot about other people. How she could send them peaches.'

'I hate peaches,' my daughter whispered to me. 'Peaches are the worst of all the fruits.'

I rested my head on her shoulder and she didn't move away.

I wondered if Agnes knew about me and felt sure, in that moment, she did. I wondered if Agnes had ever judged my mother for abandoning her child. My mother had cared for Agnes, it seemed, and Agnes had cared for her, so she had been capable of a loving relationship after all. When I was small, I had always felt there was something dark and unpredictable looming on the horizon, that no one else was paying sufficient attention and it was up to me to keep watch. I suspected, if my mother had lived with us until I was older, I might not have felt like that. When the service was over, my daughter asked if we would go to the wake – more out of interest than concern. I told her I thought not. I didn't know anyone, I wasn't feeling very well. It was strange for me, I said, to be thinking about my mother among all these people who had known her better than I had. My daughter nodded in a perfunctory way. There was music playing from somewhere, a piano piece that sounded like falling water. The room was too hot. We waited for the other people on our bench to move. As we followed them out, we got caught in the flow of mourners crossing the car park to the hotel. I couldn't bring myself to cut away, to push a path through the bodies. My daughter looked at me and I shrugged. She drained the last of her long, beige drink.

At the hotel, she ate five egg sandwiches while I had a glass of sherry.

'You're driving,' she said.

'It's just the one,' I replied. I put a dried-out sausage roll on a napkin and, after a few minutes, wrapped it up and left it on someone else's dirty plate.

'You should talk to people,' she said. 'Aren't there questions you want to ask?' She seemed frustrated. 'She was your mother,' she added, as though I might have forgotten.

I tried other formulations in my head. *She had been my mother. She hadn't been my mother.* In some ways, things weren't so different now she was dead. I drank a second glass of sherry and then we left. We drove in silence. I did feel a little drunk. The sky greyed over, then light returned. I wanted to look at everything but the road. I wanted to see the trees, the textures of leaves, the sunlight on wet tarmac. I wanted to stop and take in all the faces of the pedestrians we passed. I had felt this kind of grief before, when my father died – a kind of awakening to the world, a feeling of never having been more alive. It occurred to me that it wasn't particularly difficult to live through tragedy because, in tragedy, life simply happened to and around you. Far more difficult, far more exhausting, were the ordinary days, when it was up to you to decide what was important and what was not.

When we got home, there was a letter on the doormat. I thought perhaps it was a card, some note from a friend of my mother's sending condolences as if I had known her, as if mine were an ordinary loss. I chose not to open it right away. My daughter made another beige milkshake and went to the gym. She was there for several hours. It was pleasant to have the flat to myself of an evening. Somehow, without her, I felt less alone. I thought about all the other people who had grieved for a mother they didn't know. It was the same, perhaps, as grieving for the multitude of mothers they may have had. I would mourn the fiction of my mother, for the possibility of making fictions out of her. There would be no more fantasies of her return, of her wild apologies or explanations, or insufficient attempts to make up for lost time. There would be no opportunity now for me to say to her: *I know how it is. I have also been a mother and failed.*

I opened the note. It was from the tenants of the old stone house. They were giving notice to leave at the end of March. I still didn't have any income; I hadn't sold any paintings for a long time. When my daughter returned, drenched in sweat, I told her. She appeared delighted. It was perfect timing, she said.

'You want us to move back in?' I asked her.

'Not us,' she clarified. 'I want to live there by myself.'

Twenty-Nine

We spent a month living in my flat, time which was only made tolerable by afternoons in the studio and her obsession with the gym. In the mornings, she would do her stretches and I'd attempt to manoeuvre myself around her to get to the cereal, the bowls, the cutlery, the milk. After breakfast, feeling mean and claustrophobic, I'd go for a long walk and, when I returned, she was usually gone. Most of her time was given over to *training* though it still wasn't clear to me what the training was for. There was the gym, but there was also meditation, chanting, prayer. Sometimes I would come home to find her standing in the middle of the room, humming, with her arms outstretched. She didn't care if she was in my way. Her body hardened, solidified. She slowed down. Her muscles swelled. It seemed to me that she was, quite literally, trying to outgrow her old life. She smelled different somehow – more earthy, a little metallic. Her hair was thicker. Her mouth seemed larger. When she spoke, her voice was louder.

She made the flat look pathetic. The collapsible chairs in the kitchen could barely hold her weight. She would perch on them precariously, half supported by the strength of her legs. When we ate dinner together, she often complained that I had not made enough, unlike the friend she'd been staying with since leaving Paul. *Susie used casserole dishes. Maybe Susie could give you a recipe.* When she cooked for herself, which she preferred, it was more like a mass catering operation. She consumed whole chickens and whole lasagnes or, if we ordered in, set meals for six people. If I made a comment about any of this, she'd say: *you're right, it is surprising. The world is not designed for me.* From time to time, I broached the subject of her relationship with Paul. She never wanted to talk about it, saying that she had *moved on*. She had *fully recovered*. She had *no regrets*.

'You must have some feelings about not having regrets,' I said once. 'About any of it.'

'Yes,' she said. 'I do have some feelings,' but she did not care to say any more about them.

When the end of March came and the tenants moved out, I found I was relieved. She was right. She had to live alone. She packed her things and I drove her to the old stone house on a bright and cool early-summer afternoon. As we approached, it looked smaller than I remembered. The garden had grown up around it, there was now some ivy at the base of the walls. The bushes were wild and stringy, the grass was long. Paint peeled away in long strips from the door and the wood had cracked around the lock. I wondered what else might need doing – if the drains were blocked, if the roof was secure.

'It's perfect,' she said quietly.

I put a hand on her arm and she didn't flinch.

We crossed the lawn and peered in through the windows. I unlocked the door and we went inside. Moving slowly, we shuffled from room to room, moving slowly, examining things as if we were in a museum. Some of our furniture was still there, while other items had been placed into storage, and we tried to recall the missing pieces, like a memory game. Then she went outside. I sat down at the desk in the study and watched her lumbering around the garden, climbing the bank, putting her hand on the old tree. I thought of all the times I had watched her from this position, times she had been happy or angry or calm or disturbed. She had been so many different people in that house. It made sense that she would go there now.

Thirty

Not long after she moved back to the house, she was very unwell – a kind of flu, a vicious strain. I went to stay with her and, for a week or so, she was my little girl again. The kitchen table was back in its place, with the vast, dark-wood chair that now seemed just the right size for her. The sofa and the coffee tables and the TV cabinet had been restored to their old places in the living room. There was no bed in the master bedroom since I had taken it with me to the flat, so I slept on the sofa while she returned to her tiny childhood room.

The illness made her weak. Her muscles shrank quickly and she was sweeter to me. I made her rich soups, chicken broths with noodles and parsley, creamed potato with turmeric. I baked the kinds of bread that my father used to make. Each morning, I juiced blood oranges with ginger. One night, while I was bringing her a glass of milk, she burst into tears.

I sat with her. I touched my hand to her cheek.

'What is it?' I asked.

She threw her arms around my neck, rested the weight of her body on my shoulder. I held her close and stroked her back until she caught her breath again. She pulled away. For a brief moment, her face was completely open. She was looking at me and I was looking at her and it was twenty years ago. I thought of all the times I had tried to still her, the times I had held her in my arms after a bad dream.

'Sometimes I do think about it,' she said.

'About what?'

'About everything that happened with Paul.'

'Of course you do,' I said.

'It's the fever,' she said, resentfully. 'I've lost control.'

She told me that since she'd been unwell, in her shallow sleep she'd had visions, visitations. I suggested they were dreams, but she said no. They were more energetic than dreams, more like desires. I asked her to describe them to me and she said she couldn't, not all of them. Some of them were violent: I might not like it, I might find them upsetting. In one, there were a lot of wild creatures circling her. Her only method of defence was to be as still as possible, to make them think she was not a person but something more permanent, like a building or a tree. But she could never be still enough; they came for her.

'It's all right if you haven't recovered,' I said. 'You don't have to recover from everything.'

She held my gaze. Light spilled through the blinds in the

bedroom, hazy and warm. She turned away to keep it out of her eyes.

'It doesn't matter what he did.'

'Of course it does.'

'No,' she said. 'You don't understand. It matters what I do. As far as I'm concerned, he didn't do anything. I did something. I made the change.'

It cost her some effort to explain this. She had raised her voice. Her cheeks were flushed. Afterwards, she needed rest, she slept for eighteen hours. She only woke up to drink water, litres of it, fortified with sugar and salt. She drenched her sheets in sweat.

The next morning, she felt better again and she asked me to leave.

Thirty-One

We continued to talk on the phone. I sensed that she didn't particularly want to but perhaps did so from a sense of gratitude: I had given her the house. She understood what this meant for me, the precarious position in which I found myself. During one of our conversations, I said I'd been thinking about how, when she was at university, we used to talk for hours. She had always asked about what I'd done and where I'd been and was keen to know how I passed the time. For a time, she had worried about me and given me advice, but now she never asked.

'That's true,' she observed coolly. 'We used to talk a lot.'

There followed a lengthy explanation of the ways in which the rhythms of our relationship had been permanently changed. She made no attempt to comfort me in this. All she wanted was to be perfectly clear. Her reasoning was thus: because she loved me so much, I was a terrible drain on her energy. She had learned to think of her energy as a precious and meaningful thing, and I told her she was right about that.

'Good for you,' I said.

It wasn't healthy, she told me. She was investing in herself, now. She couldn't be wasting her talents on others.

'So we won't talk?' I asked her. 'I can't visit my own house?'

She said of course I would be able to visit. I owned the house. It was my legal right, only I had to give her twenty-four hours' notice. Then she said that she was pleased to have had the chance to explain and was glad that I had understood. It was time for her to train, she would have to go.

At that point, she had only published one or two videos. She was still at the beginning of her new career. I found it moving to see her do something so effortful and make it look like nothing. I was proud of her sensibilities, her composition, the delicacy of it all. At the same time, I didn't quite know what I was watching. It wasn't immediately clear to me who it was for. What one person might think of as meditation, another might see as performance art. More confusing to me still was the platform on which the videos were published, which included a lot of loud and ugly advertisements, a lot of links to other videos making an ugly square pattern across the screen. It seemed wrong to experience her beautiful work in this way, where it was often rudely interrupted, where it was quite impossible to enter any kind of meditative state. But she knew how it worked. When she started making money and paying rent, I did not complain.

*

The last time I went to the house, it was my birthday. I'd asked to see her. To my surprise, she agreed. She gave me specific instructions about when I could come and how long I could stay. For a few days, I was nervous. I braced myself for her rejections, her dismissals. At the same time, I longed to be near her; that early sensation of always wanting to hold her when she was so small had never entirely disappeared. She knew this, I think. To her, it probably seemed like weakness, but to me, it was my own feat of endurance.

Some parts of the house had changed. The master bedroom was being used as a studio, and she'd set up her bench press in the study. The garden remained overgrown, but in a wild and beautiful way. There were various props set up on the lawn: a thick rope, a golden ball, a rubber strap, a stone sculpture, pampas grass, a Victorian parasol. The camera tripod stood next to the tree. The studio seemed vast. I couldn't recall my bedroom ever feeling so large, but without the bed, the wardrobe and the dressing table it was wide open and full of light. There were all manner of plants and fabrics in there, things she could move in and out of shot so that each of her videos was aesthetically distinct. In one corner, there was a desktop computer and a rattan chair where she edited her work. By the window, there was a large wooden chest. She was busy in the kitchen, blending frozen mango with chia seeds and something else. I opened the chest slowly. I don't know what I expected to find. There were a couple of yoga mats, swathes of fabric and the handheld Tibetan bells she liked. There were the blankets I had given her when she went to university. There was a framed picture of me sitting in the garden. There were poems she had written in school, university essays. There were teenage posters and teenage diaries, a dried flower, a commemorative coin. Her favourite books were wrapped up in a pink sheet. Beneath them was *The Whirligig* video cassette, the old tape player and a tangle of headphones. I opened the tape player, carefully. Miss Tamm's tape was still there, wound back to the start. I looked at the materials of her childhood. She hadn't rejected her old life after all, I thought. She was repurposing it.

Thirty-Two

The oil paintings are almost finished. They are vast and they are hideous, by far the best work I've ever done. A new gallery in Sheffield will host the exhibition. My favourite piece is one that shows two strangers in an argument. Apparent on their faces – contorted, frozen in time – is the difficulty of feeling anger towards someone you don't know. True anger is usually reserved for our most intimate relationships. I wrote to my daughter to tell her about the exhibition, though she hated the paintings and we never speak anymore. The last contact we had, she told me that she was *going quiet*. She wanted to see what it did for her well-being. Though I don't expect a reply, I feel closer to her having shared my news. I feel sure she has read the message, which means that, at least for a moment, she thought of me.

The mother of the missing young man continues to write. Her emails are loquacious and informative. She tells me about her son, the kind of person he is, how he never had many friends, what he was like as a child. It was difficult to raise him, she told me, because she had separated from his father, who was not a nice man, often angry and unkind. Most recently, she wrote to say that her son had been featured on the local news; perhaps I had seen the report. She was disappointed that my daughter's videos were not mentioned, not least because other people were missing now, too. My daughter was a dangerous person, she said. What, she wanted to know, was I going to do?

I read the comments on her latest videos. In among the posts about her beauty and her strength, her *inner peace*, there were a few hysterical messages, probably left by the same woman who'd been writing to me. I called the landline in the old stone house. I wasn't angry with her, I wanted to know what she thought. Was her message really dangerous? Did she have so much influence? Did she really want other people to abandon their family and friends? I sat in the kitchen. The fridge hummed. Orange light beamed in through the window above the sink and cut a stripe across the table. If she answered the phone, I would be able to invite her again to the exhibition. I would be able to say sorry again, to tell her again that I loved her. It would be a joy to hear her voice, to have her there, in the present, with me. If she answered, I might not even mention the missing son, because what was he to us, after all?

III

SUSIE

One

She came to stay with me after the break-up. She arrived in late September and left again in late March. During the dark half of the year, she hibernated, and by the time she emerged, she was changed. It might have seemed that I was doing her a favour – giving her a place to stay, keeping her safe – but really it was the other way around. For months, I'd had a nervous, bubbling feeling, and for a while, when she moved in, it disappeared.

I'd known her for several years. The three of us – me, her and Paul – had joined the firm at the same time. In the beginning, the work was confusing; I was learning to do things I didn't understand. I made notes, contributed to meetings, and everything seemed to be going well, but at the end of the day, I'd look back on what I'd written and think: I don't know what those words mean. I watched her and Paul carefully to see if they might have the same feeling. Early on, I could tell that Paul did not. He was shy, a little awkward, but the general environment agreed with him. He acquired the language of the office quickly, it seemed to move through him in a natural way. Once he gained confidence, other people responded to him as if he were handsome, though I never thought he was. Conversely, she was beautiful, which no one else appeared to see.

I spent a lot of time looking at her. Her hair came down over her shoulders in thick waves, and she tucked it into the back of her shirt when she ate. She was difficult to talk to, unafraid of silence, often pausing a long while before she spoke. If you asked her a question, she'd answer succinctly and hold your gaze a beat too long. When she did speak, her hands made broad curves through the air, as though not entirely under her control. She became friendly with the administrators, the secretaries and the interns. She refused the power games of the office, which made it easy to underestimate her, though I should have known better. In that firm, all the women were spectacular – smart and funny and composed. The men were, by contrast, ridiculous – wearing expensive socks embroidered with cartoons and doing triathlons at weekends.

The first time I worked with her on a case, I was anxious about it. She didn't appear to understand what other people expected of her, but I was wrong about that: she didn't care. Unlike her, I had always done everything that was expected of me. I tried to look smart, clothes carefully pressed, hair pinned in a neat bun. My make-up was precise, a thin black line around the eyes, or a clean red lip. I wore black-rimmed glasses and pencil skirts with stylish, uncomfortable shoes. Though I'd lived all my life in the north of England, I'd learned to speak with an undetectable, non-regional accent, so that no one could be sure if I was Northern or Southern, or even from overseas. I was careful to present myself as the right kind of person for any given situation and, for a long time, I was convinced that everyone lived that way – trying hard to do the right thing while pretending not to try at all. It had never occurred to me that there might be something powerful, profitable even, in being exactly who you were.

On our first day in court together, I thought she wasn't going to show up. When at last she arrived, she was in a terrible state. Her hair was tangled and knotted at her neck, held roughly in place by an elastic band. Her skirt didn't fit, her blazer wasn't ironed, a tissue was slipping from the cuff of her sleeve. I went to help her with the files and, as I held out my arms to take them, she tripped and fell, jabbing them into my stomach.

'Sorry,' she said, flustered, a little sweaty, out of breath.

I smiled and tried to act as if it hadn't hurt.

Our clients had all witnessed our undignified entrance: the trip, the spilled papers, two young women struggling to arrange their bodies in a reasonable way. At the time, I felt humiliated – I was sure they would never take us seriously after that. Now, I suspect she did it on purpose: a theatrical manoeuvre, a clever prologue.

I don't remember the specifics of that case, there have

been many other cases since, but I do remember watching her and feeling a small thrill. It wasn't to do with what she was saying – that was predetermined, more or less – but how she said it: calm, smiling, relaxed. Her energy had a peculiar effect, nobody expected it from her. Because, while she was speaking, she appeared so much at ease, her arguments seemed to be drawn irrefutably from a place of truth. If she wanted to check something, she apologised gloriously and looked at her notes. When something seemed funny to her, she threw back her head and she laughed. She did not adopt the persona of a lawyer, which was the only thing I'd learned to do. Instead, her own innate mannerisms, her seemingly authentic and unrehearsed responses, were more effective than any behaviour she might have acquired through practice and effort. She knew this, she used it and we won. I left the courtroom feeling slightly different about myself. I vowed to be less afraid to talk in my own voice, or to follow my own line of thought, though I had no clear sense of either of these things. I wanted to learn how to be myself again, having been carefully unlearning it ever since I was born.

I started seeking her out in the office. I noted the coffee she liked to drink, the Japanese café she preferred for lunch, the little shop where she stopped to buy art supplies after work. When it transpired that we were spending a lot of time together, she began to treat me as her friend and I experienced this as a kind of achievement, a sign of my own personal progress. It wasn't something I'd thought about much before, perhaps because I hadn't met many others, but I considered her *a good person*, someone I trusted to bring goodness to my life.

There was a coffee shop near the office where we often ate breakfast together. I liked to get there first, so I could watch her come in, so that her day would start with seeing me, as if before then it hadn't really begun. We talked about work, which she treated lightly, which hardly seemed to affect her at all. Sometimes we touched on more personal things. I told her about my strange feeling, that sometimes words felt foreign to me, and she nodded as if it made sense. Over time, I got used to her long silences, I even found them comforting. That was her version of intimacy, I thought. It didn't occur to me that she was still being careful, that there were many things I didn't know.

When she finally told me about her and Paul, I was surprised and a little hurt. I hadn't realised that, if she wasn't at work or with me, she was often with him. She had never talked about Paul, or any previous boyfriends. If she'd been looking for a relationship, she'd never mentioned it. I can't remember what I said to her at the time. I remember feeling quite unwell. They seemed such an odd match, I started to worry what other fundamental things I might have misunderstood about the people I knew. I wondered how it had begun, with after-work drinks, or a restaurant date. Had she felt butterflies, did he make her nervous? Was she falling in love? The vocabulary felt all wrong, I couldn't make the words stick. It seemed to me that she was using him for something – an experiment, to exercise some neurosis – but after they moved in together, I accepted it was serious. She had chosen Paul.

We stopped meeting at the coffee shop. I still saw her, but it was different. We'd go for lunch or a drink, or she invited me over when Paul wasn't there, to watch a film or to look at her new paintings, which were always large and somehow naive. She must have known I didn't like him. Paul and I understood things so differently – he was certain about everything, while it all felt dangerously provisional to me. Once or twice, I heard him undermine her at work. He liked to suggest that she wasn't doing her fair share, that other people had to compensate for her. He didn't sound angry, or even judgemental, so when he said these things, they felt true. I wanted to tell her but didn't know how. I missed the conspiratorial feeling of our pre-work breakfasts, where it felt as though we weren't just friends or colleagues, but something more singular and focused, allies in an invisible war.

I continued going to the coffee shop, without her. I told the waitress that my friend had moved to the suburbs, and she smiled sympathetically. When a different waitress appeared one day, I told her too, but she didn't care. After that, I stopped going. A few months later, the whole place closed down. For the most part, life carried on as it had before, but it felt duller, monotone, like I was travelling through an endless landscape, beige roads, beige fields. I wanted something on the horizon – a jagged mountain, a gaping ravine.

Two

Since starting at the firm, I'd saved up a lot of money. I didn't like to think of all that cash just sitting there. I imagined all the people who would be grateful to have it, who would know how to use it to improve their lives. It felt absurd to me that there was nothing I really wanted, as if by not wanting anything I wasn't a real person. It seemed I was waiting for something, permission maybe, but from whom? In a panic, I bought a flat with a huge deposit and moved in right away.

It was a big, light-filled, hollow kind of place. The estate agent, Fiona, had referred to it as *minimalist* but really it was avant-garde. Large, steel-framed windows cut the walls at jaunty angles. Tall steps demarcated the kitchen, the dining area and the lounge so that, while the effect was open-plan, you still had to watch where you were going. It was styled like an urban art gallery – rough walls, exposed concrete, pale and gleaming tiles on the floor. Fiona made an easy sell.

She kept telling me it was a buyer's market and I believed her because I wanted to.

'You're amazing!' said Fiona. 'So decisive! There aren't many women who operate like that.'

But I wasn't being decisive, I was scared. Some old friends had moved out of the city to raise their children in the countryside; others had quit their graduate jobs to do the things they actually liked. I had a strange, numb feeling, like nothing was real. I was drinking more than usual and working stranger hours. There were days when I obsessed over the details of a case, staying up half the night, and there were other days where I could hardly concentrate at all. At first, I thought the problem was physical, and I committed to various regimes – no sugar, intermittent fasting, nil by mouth after 6 p.m. – but before I could see if they had any effect, I'd get drunk and forget and order a takeaway late at night. I hoped the move would shake me out of my stuck feelings. I craved change because it seemed a reasonable sub-stitute for progress. I'd spent all my money in one fat lump, I'd moved out of my perfectly pleasant rental. In a different environment, I thought, I'd be free to become someone new, or to feel like my old self, whichever was more appealing at the time.

The flat was part of a small complex of converted ware-houses, each with tilted rhombus windows, as though the building had been picked up and shaken, the key components knocked out of line. I was the first to move in – the others took a long time to sell. When I came home from work, I'd walk down my deserted street, enter the key code for my deserted building, and sit by myself in my vast grey box where I could hear the sound of my own breathing knocking around the walls. Sometimes, at weekends, I heard Fiona showing people around the neighbouring apartments. I heard them tripping over the unexpected steps, cursing loudly. Once she had a guy whose voice seemed to crash through the whole building, and I prayed he wouldn't move in. I heard Fiona start to warn him. *Mind the—* And then came the thud. *Ha!* he boomed. *Who the hell put that there?* Fiona laughed a little nervous laugh. *Part of the charm!* she quipped. *Part of the original architecture, back when the building was—* The man laughed again, a loud and cruel sound. He told Fiona to save her time. I watched him walk down the street to his car, jabbing fingers at his phone. I wondered if he was telling his friends about it, what he might say, the words he would use. I wondered when I might finally invite someone over, which was another way of wondering when I'd finally admit that I'd made a mistake.

One morning, after a terrible night's sleep, I tripped on one of the steps myself. I'd woken too early, feeling as though I hadn't slept at all. I filled the kettle and spooned coffee into the drip filter, as usual. The cereal box was empty, the bread had grown a crust of mould, the only item in the fruit bowl was a sad, wrinkled lime. I poured the water into the filter, balanced it over a large mug and walked to the table by the window, where the sun was tipping over the skyline and into the day. I forgot the step and fell. Scalding water spilled over my arm, the mug fell to the floor and smashed, coffee grounds scattered in damp clumps. As I got up, I hit my head on the table and the pain was hard and deep. I ran to the bathroom and put my arm under the tap. When the heat ran out, I looked up and saw the cut on my forehead, the drip-trail of blood down my face and neck. I washed and dressed, then arranged my hair to hide the cut. I was late for work. When I came home that evening, I returned to the mess of coffee and shattered porcelain on the floor.

I hated the flat. The vast slanted windows looked out over the old factories and the light streamed in, even when it was overcast. It felt exposing, all that light. I tried to avoid it but the angles were unpredictable, you could step out of the beams but there was still the reflective glare. The ceilings were high and any noise – the scrape of a chair, the rattle of cutlery in a closing drawer – seemed to linger a long time. The whole place felt cold and unforgiving, as though it wasn't designed for a human, but for a harder, more durable creature – a robot, or an athlete. The furniture I bought made it worse still. The stainless-steel dining table was too big and ostentatious for me to eat there by myself. The dining chairs were tall-backed metal constructions that, when I sat in them, made me feel as if someone were standing right behind me. Before she came to stay with me, I ate dinner on the sofa. When I'd finished, I'd put my plate on the floor, wrap a blanket over my shoulders and watch television on my laptop until it was time to go to bed. I hated loading the dishwasher, so the plates just sat there next to the sofa, piled on the corner of an expensive green rug. At night, when I got undressed, I left my clothes in a heap.

At first, the mess made the place seem friendlier and less austere, but the cumulative effect was depressing. It seemed to me I was a kind of squatter, killing time until the real owners of the apartment returned. I started staying late at work to avoid having to spend any time at home. I walked back instead of taking the bus, which took over an hour, and on the way I'd pick up something to eat – discount sandwiches, salad boxes, or whatever was left of the deli counter. I thought about selling the place on again and buying somewhere else – a cosier flat, a small house, a Victorian terrace with friendly neighbours – but I couldn't face the expense or the paperwork or the accompanying sense of personal failure.

I don't think I was depressed in a medical sense, but sometimes it's hard to say precisely where circumstances end and chemical imbalances begin. When I spoke to my clients, I always felt I was repeating myself, as if we never made any progress but were simply having the same conversation again and again. We'd arrange a meeting, I'd send an email confirmation, and then we'd talk and I'd confirm again by email that we had. I got a promotion, which sounded like a good thing, though our boss told me several times that it was a big responsibility and I started to feel I was, in fact, being punished. They were giving me an assistant, which seemed another clear sign that they thought I wouldn't cope. Sometimes, when I ought to have been working, I made excuses – doctor's appointments, family emergencies – and left early to drink by myself. I thought: I've already been promoted, what can they do? I thought: I'm too senior to get away with this now, I'll surely get sacked.

Then one afternoon, I found her in the break room in a terrible state. I didn't recognise her immediately. I was tired, having accidentally drifted off on the sofa the night before. My vision was blurry and momentarily I mistook her for one of the clients – someone in the middle of a humiliating divorce or a medical negligence case. But then I saw the mass of hair tucked into the back of her shirt. I sat down next to her and put my arm around her shoulders. She started to shake, so I moved away.

'I can't help it,' she said.

'That's all right,' I replied.

Her feet were knocking against the legs of her chair. She folded her arms tightly against her chest.

'Is there anything I can do?' I asked.

She took a deep breath, then she drew herself towards me and nestled her head in the crook of my neck. I smelled the shampoo in her hair; her skin felt hot beneath her clothes.

'Do you want to talk about it?' I said.

Her whole body contracted then, curling in on itself like a dead bug. I wrapped both arms around her and she sobbed. We stayed like that for a while, then when she recovered herself she said: 'Susie, I'm going to need somewhere to stay.'

That afternoon, I left work at an appropriate time. I washed and dried the dishes and stacked them neatly in the cupboards. I loaded the dirty laundry into the machine and made up the guest bed in bright, patterned sheets. At the supermarket, I stocked up on good and wholesome foods: eggs, apricots, garlic, crème fraîche, expensive muesli, salted butter, Dutch cheeses, dark chocolate, rice noodles, butter beans, dried chickpeas, gochujang. I bought some plants and dotted them around the windows. Then I went back to the supermarket and bought a bottle of vodka, a bag of ice and some wine. When she arrived, I helped her haul an enormous suitcase up the stairs. It was heavy and the zips were straining, it wouldn't quite close at one end. She really was leaving him then, I thought. It was over for her and Paul. I watched as she unpacked some of her things and, when she wasn't looking at me, I smiled. I lit a candle, poured drinks, shook crisps into a bowl. I slid the switch to dim the lights.

'This place is amazing,' she said, walking back into the living room.

I looked around and saw she was right. The evening light pooled in, golden and complex. The kitchen gleamed. One of the new plants was starting to open a flower. She stretched herself out on the sofa and her sad, tired face was very beautifully arranged. She sighed and I went to sit next to her, resting my arm on top of her arm. In that moment, I felt normal. I finally felt I had a grip on myself.

Three

At first, she was signed off sick, then she took a few weeks of annual leave. After that, she handed in her notice – or, rather, I did it on her behalf. I didn't know what she was going to do, and didn't like to ask, in case she felt pressured, or mistook the question as a sign of my wanting her to leave.

While she lived with me, I had a better life. In the evenings, she would meditate or read her wellness magazines, while I read novels for the first time in years. As soon as I got to the end of one book, I opened the next without thinking. I followed the lives of the characters without caring about them at all. They moved like shadows in the back of my mind and when the story was over, I never thought of it again. There wasn't much space for anyone besides her, no matter if they were real or not. My clients no longer kept me up at night. The moment I left the office, they vanished without trace.

I hired a cleaner to come twice a week and bought fresh

flowers at the weekends. I made elaborate, wholesome meals by following recipes I found online. I read the steps carefully, with the kind of concentration usually reserved for work. Mostly, the food was delicious. She kept telling me not to go to such trouble, but I wanted to go to the trouble, and for her to feel the weight of the gesture, too. *It's a nice thing,* I told her. *I used to cook for my family, and now I'm cooking for you.* This was a half-truth, making it sound like the same thing, because when I cooked for my brothers I didn't care at all and they never thanked me for it either. I revelled in her gratitude. *This is amazing,* she would gush. *I feel like you're nursing me back to health.* When she said things like this, I'd feel a kind of glow all over my body, a warm patch on my back as if someone's hand was there. I paid close attention to what she seemed to like best and what she left on her plate. She loved pomegranate seeds, asparagus and cauliflower, and anything made with fresh coriander or mint. She

could eat mountains of pasta and rice. I served everything with bread, an artisanal sourdough that she devoured. We had side dishes of avocado, buttered kale and samphire. Her appetite suffered nothing in the name of her broken heart. She started to look extraordinarily healthy, with bright skin and high colour in her cheeks. I couldn't understand it – I was eating all the same food that she was, albeit in smaller quantities, but my skin remained dull and dry. Over dinner, we listened to music and talked about the news or the things we'd read. She was often affectionate, kissing me on the cheek before bed, and sometimes in the morning as I left for work.

With her there, I found I had stepped into the kind of life I'd always hoped for but had never arrived at on my own. I wanted her to be happy, I tried to support all the changes she made. I witnessed her transformation, physical and psychic, and was mesmerised, like everyone else. But I never wanted her to leave. I wanted to come home to her always, for us to live like that forever.

Four

Little by little, she revealed to me the truth of her relationship with Paul. At first, she only hinted obliquely that he had not always treated her well. I assumed, rather unimaginatively, that he must have been having an affair, with someone younger and more obviously beautiful. But it wasn't an affair, it was darker and stranger than that. As the days went by, she filled in the details and I learned all about the little room where he shut her up for long periods, sometimes not even giving her anything to eat or drink.

She explained her survival strategies calmly – the hidden toothbrush, the notebooks, the snacks. I'd been to their house a few times, so I could picture it all very easily – her tall body hunched up on the floor, the sound of the television rising up from downstairs. When she described it to me, she sounded curious, a little puzzled, as though trying to piece it all together. She wasn't angry or upset. It was as if she had already removed herself from the memory so that, in talking about what happened to her, she could feel as if she were making it up.

Paul avoided me in the office. He asked to be transferred to the London branch, and management refused. He got thinner, his skin became lined, but his work didn't suffer; if anything he was more successful than before. We didn't have any cases together at that time, but I heard other people talking about his brilliant performances in court, his ruthless tactics, his quick thinking and sharp delivery. When we did run into each other, I tried to remain professional. She had asked me not to say anything to him. I wanted her to report him, not just at work but to the police. It never happened. He had taken enough from her, she said. She wouldn't give him any more of her energy, she wouldn't waste any more of her time on him.

In meetings, I found myself staring at Paul, tracing the shape of his face and guessing at the

contents of his thoughts. Was he thinking about her? Did he know that I knew? He had a square head but a weak jaw. I'd never really considered the geometry of his appearance before, but now I saw that his eyes were small and unsymmetrical, the left larger than the right. Because they were set so deep into his face, they made his nose seem disproportionate, his forehead a wide plain. His expressions were often mechanical, as though he were only practising real feelings, trying them out until one of them stuck. Sometimes he'd catch my eye and I'd steel myself and hold his gaze. The more I looked at him, the more subhuman he appeared. It was clear that I made him nervous. When we passed in the hallways or at one of the coffee machines, he would only mumble *hello*. I was pleased he could never look me in the eye for too long – it meant that he knew I was loyal to her.

Occasionally, other people in the office would ask me how she was. When she quit, they'd been surprised, and later a few of them had made judgements about whether or not she'd ever been cut out for law. I told them all that she was doing fine, that she was taking some time to think, but really I had no idea. I knew she had a plan, or she had told me as much, but from what I had seen, she was spending her days in the flat watching yoga videos and reading wellness magazines. When I came home in the evenings, laden with groceries, she didn't want to hear about work. I would ask if she'd had a nice day and she would smile warmly and say that she had. Sometimes she'd tell me about an article she'd read or demonstrate the advanced asana she had practised. *Today I meditated for thirty minutes*, she'd say. *Today I meditated for two hours*. I'd smile encouragingly, then she'd ask me what was for dinner. *Thank you for having me, Susie*, she would say, or: *Susie, you're an angel*, and my heart swelled. At work, I counted down the hours and then the minutes until I would see her again. While I waited for the bus in the evenings, I tapped my boots on the tarmac or rocked back and forth on my heels. What would she be doing when I got there? Would she be reading on the sofa? Would she be lying on the bed? Would she be stretching by the window or meditating on the rug? I was always impatient to see her. If the bus took too long to come, I'd call a cab.

Once I came back and found her ticking boxes on a magazine quiz: *What kind of wellness plant are you?* She asked me to sit with her. The questions were things like: *How would you describe your personal growth? A: I change with the wind. B: Slow and steady, I'm putting down roots. C: I can survive almost anywhere with nothing.* She got *Passionflower!* I got *Dandelion!* She was *expensive, soothing, an aid to relaxation*; I was *resilient, a stimulant for the liver.* At the end of the quiz there were recipe suggestions. *Are you Passionflower? Try muesli with crystallised ginger. Are you Dandelion? Why not add cold rice to your soup?*

I didn't share any of her interests. Meditation sounded like torture to me. I never thought consciously about how I was breathing, I couldn't sit still for more than five minutes. Even while reading or watching television, I'd often find myself clacking my teeth, working my jaw from side to side. Once or twice, while we were sitting on the sofa together, she reached out and put a hand to my cheek. 'Don't do that,' she'd say. She'd massage my cheeks and we'd both laugh and afterwards I'd do as I'd been told.

Five

To make the flat more comfortable for her, I bought all kinds of things. There were blankets and large cushions with organic cotton covers; there were room sprays and essential oils. I hung pictures I thought she'd like: abstract, geometric shapes in what seemed to me like meditative colours – blues and greens and mauves. In the kitchen, there were a range of gadgets to facilitate the making of herbal tea – glass pots, strainers, infusers, imbuers and something called a *tea stick*. In the bathroom, there were jade rollers, sugar scrubs, seed oils and cleansing salts. There was a madly expensive yoga mat. It had been beautifully displayed in the window of a fitness shop, next to a yucca plant and some church candles. As soon as I saw it, I pictured her on it, moving in her new, slow way. The shop girl told me it was made from recycled bottles and sustainable tree rubber. She wouldn't sell me the plant but threw in a couple of candles for free. While at work, I often thought about that mat, the squishy dark green surface of it. *She's touching it,* I thought. *She is pressing her hands against it. She has lain her body there.* Once, she told me there were toxic chemicals in shampoo, so I found a recipe online, lemon juice and coconut oil shaken up in a jar. If she found something she wanted in a magazine, she would leave the page open in the kitchen for me to see. Whatever it was, whatever it cost, I would buy it, unwrap it and put it out for her to use.

There were times when she appeared so self-assured and calm, it was as if nothing bad had ever happened to her. At other moments, I'd find her trembling, hunched over, inconsolably sad. She told me how she used to get the shakes as a little girl. She was a nervous child, she said, until a teacher had taught her to sit still. Every day I learned something new about her childhood, about her mother, the stone house where they lived. She remembered the shapes of the cracks in the paintwork, the colour of the paving in the garden path. Sometimes I wondered if she was regressing, forcing herself to move backward through time until she could get to a point where there had never been any Paul.

She became more serious about her exercise routine. At first, it was an hour of yoga in the morning, an hour and a half in the afternoon, a meditation in the evening. Later on, it was yoga at sunrise, followed by several hours in the gym, a long afternoon spent in silent contemplation and an evening of stretching so that she'd be able to walk the next day. The rest of the time, she watched videos online – a digital walk through a Japanese garden, a documentary about ancient woodlands, time-lapse sunrises and sunsets, ASMR role plays. She was selective about the kinds of content she consumed. She was working on her inner landscape, she told me, weeding out anything she didn't need.

Each day, she looked a little different – stronger, shinier, more truly herself. First thing – while she stood in the kitchen, draped in a linen dressing gown, waiting for some herbal concoction to infuse – she looked like an ancient statue, a warrior goddess rendered in stone. In the evenings, I often took pictures of her. She enjoyed arranging her body in aesthetically pleasing ways, and she was good at it, too. In real life, it looked very uncomfortable, but the pictures turned out beautifully – the deranged windows were a nice backdrop. Her body would appear silhouetted against the bright sunset, her muscles bulging, her head tilted, her mouth slightly open. If the weather was dull, her skin would look radiant, her cheeks flushed pink. I would see her dark lashes and the wetness in her eyes. There were so many shapes in her body; everything was an angle or a whole. Sometimes at night, when we were both in bed, I'd find myself thinking of the shapes the camera couldn't see. What did the insides of her ears look like? Or the gaps between her toes?

Six

At the end of October, she developed her own style of meditation. I remember because the shops along the street where I waited for the bus had garish window displays – fake pumpkins, green masks, witch hats, kitten ears. I've always hated Halloween. It's not the trick-or-treaters or the horror films or the thinning veil between worlds: it's the plastic and the nylon and the neon tulle. Halloween arrives as an abundance of flammable materials, cheap and indestructible, a recurring ecological nightmare.

Every year, I think about a party I went to when I was small. My older cousin dressed me up in too-big clothes and then lowered a large white clown mask over my face. It had plastic arms, like a pair of glasses, and the harsh, serrated edge dug into the skin behind my ear. I hadn't wanted to go, but my cousin said it would be good for me to have some fun, and my parents agreed. I was a quiet and serious child, nobody listened to my protestations and in the end I had no choice. At a certain point in the evening, I touched my hand to my hair and my fingers came away covered in blood. I screamed. A few people looked at me, then laughed. The mask had cut through the skin behind my ear. My cousin thought it was a joke, a Halloween trick, but when half an hour went by and I had not stopped crying she took me home. She was very disappointed. She wouldn't invite me anywhere again, she said, not to her birthday party, not even to her sister's First Communion. We walked back and I saw the dark, damp world through a lens of tears. The wound behind my ear had stopped bleeding, but it still felt as if something was in there, a little bug burrowing into the skull. When we got home, I saw myself in the mirror that hung in the porch. On one side, my hair was matted and congealed. My mother rinsed it out and I watched the sickly, orange water pool in the sink then twist down the plughole. She told me my brothers would have been glad to go to a party

like that, if only they were old enough. She said that nice experiences were wasted on me. The clown face went into the bin, but I still think of it. Plastic takes four hundred and fifty years to decompose, so the mask still exists: somewhere in a mountain of trash is the face of a clown with a bloodstained edge.

I considered all this while waiting for the bus after work. A woman standing nearby had a shiny witch costume poking out of a carrier bag; another held a stack of green plastic cups. When the bus arrived, I found a seat by a window and slid open the glass panel. A man behind me sighed loudly and moved to another seat but nobody asked me to close it again. I breathed in the cold, damp air. It smelled of petrol and smoke but sometimes also of wet leaves – it was the stage of autumn where everything dissolves into the earth. As I walked down the empty streets towards home, the pavements glistened. The street lights were amber and beautiful and, perhaps for the first time, I felt glad to live in a deserted, post-industrial complex, where there would be no Halloween parties, no trick-or-treaters, no abandoned masks to clog up the gutters. As I approached, the only light in the building came from my flat. The blinds were open and I could see all of her, her body dark against the glow of the lamp. I watched. She was standing very still, her arms made a perfect *V*, her face and palms turned up towards the ceiling. It looked as if she were asking some vast, universal question, as if, at any moment, a divine answer might come from above. I must have stood there a long time. When I finally looked away, my hands were numb with cold, and a light rain had dampened my hair. It was like seeing an apparition. If anyone else had passed by, they might have mistaken her for an image – a cardboard cut-out, a giant ghost.

I tiptoed up the stairs and opened the door as softly as I could.

She did not turn.

'Hello,' I whispered.

Silence.

I put down my bag, stepped out of my shoes, slipped off

my jacket and stretched my arms. They ached from the day's work. My neck was always stiff. Compared to her, I felt malformed. She was so much at ease, perfectly balanced and poised. Perhaps this is why so many people admire her – most of us can only aspire to that kind of grace.

I adjusted the position of the lamp and she didn't seem to notice. I took some photographs on my phone. When the images appeared on the little screen it looked as if she were made of bronze, the light hitting the swell of her muscles and then giving way to the curve of shadow beneath. I poured myself a glass of wine. Time passed; I was absorbed in my watching. I thought about the various components of her – the colours, lines, textures and shapes – as if she were only a collection of surfaces. Then she moved. Her composure fell away instantly. Suddenly, she was out of breath. She stretched her arms one way and then the other, she made circular movements with her wrists. At last, she came to sit with me on the sofa, thumping herself down on it with such force that my own body jerked to one side.

'What were you doing?' I asked.

She cracked her neck.

'Practising,' she said.

'You looked very graceful,' I told her. I showed her the pictures and she nodded. I said how beautiful she was, then she asked me to airdrop the pictures to her.

'I'm hungry,' she said. 'Have you cooked?'

I shook my head. I hadn't wanted to disturb her, clattering pots and pans in the kitchen.

She sighed.

We ordered Japanese, enough for five people. She ate two bowls of ramen, a tofu katsu and ten gyoza. We'd ordered so much food that they'd sent us free desserts – a custard pancake sandwich and three flavours of mochi. She ate those too. I lifted up my noodles and put them back down again. We didn't talk. I watched her eat. Each spoonful commanded her full attention as if she had forgotten I was there.

'Are you all right?' I asked her.

There was no reply.

'Are you warm enough?' I tried.

She looked at me through narrowed eyes and gave a fraction of a nod. She started to get very tired. Her eyes drifted shut and then opened again, her breathing became heavy and loud. I told her she should just go to bed. When I put an arm around her, she leaned on my shoulder and sobbed. We sat together like that for several long minutes, and when I looked up again the street lights had gone out.

'I'll make you a hot-water bottle,' I offered.

She said no. She turned to face me, looking quite different, much softer and younger somehow, then she asked if I might tuck her in. She changed into pyjamas, washed her face, brushed her teeth and climbed into bed. I tucked the duvet all the way round, so you could see the full shape of her under the covers. I gathered it up at her shoulders and pressed it firmly around her neck. She closed her eyes, her mouth opened slightly. She looked dead. I felt blissful. I sat with her, stroking her hair, until she was fast asleep.

Seven

These days, she makes a living out of standing still for a long time. She doesn't live in the city anymore, she's moved back to her childhood home. Perhaps her devoted followers picture her living in an eco-haven, a whitewashed house by the beach or some rugged paradise on the moors. Or perhaps they imagine her in a different country altogether, somewhere with clearer skies and warmer air. She's good at filming things in the right light, at the right time of day. Watching her videos, you'd never know that she lives in a dilapidated cottage next to a railway station car park.

Mostly, she films in the garden, which is large and grown wild. It's cleverly laid out, with strategically placed grasses and potted shrubs so that it's hard to get a sense of where it starts and ends. She regularly changes her props. Sometimes the garden isn't even recognisable as a garden, and instead looks like the forest, or wild grassland. The videos themselves are very beautiful. She styles her hair carefully and chooses clothes that subtly accentuate her appearance. She has a soft, ochre sweater the same colour as her eyes; there's a sea-green dress that makes her hair look more golden, her skin brighter and her teeth white. The aesthetic is consistent, recognisable. It reproduces something of her paintings, which were large and figurative – wobbly, skeleton shapes with splashes of brightness emerging from unexpected parts, a single bone made luminous, or the soles of the feet, or the inner corner of an eye. There was a translucent quality to the subjects she painted – they seemed to suggest that, if you looked closely enough, you might be able to locate the source, the bright and pulsing thing that made them real. These days, she too appears translucent, as if she has taken the feeling of her paintings and drawn it into herself. Though I see the work that goes into the videos – how staged they are, how carefully produced – whatever she does, it still feels true.

In the first one I saw – one of the first she released – she stands before the camera with her arms wide open. Her body is made to seem bare and vulnerable, but at the same time she looks strong. My eyes were drawn to the lines of her neck, to the insides of her wrists, to her décolletage, where the skin appeared thinner and less opaque. I felt some discomfort around those areas of my own body, too, as if I were about to become very ill. My chest tightened, my shoulders tensed. Suddenly I was cold when before I'd been warm. I felt like people were watching me, when really, I was at home with the door locked.

The video begins with an empty shot of the garden. In the middle of the frame is a big, old tree. There's a breeze and the leaves are rustling, the light is a good, late-spring light. For a while, it's just this, the tree and the light and the sound of the breeze crackling into the microphone. Then she appears, walking into the frame from the left and moving, very slowly, to stand in front of the trunk. For a few moments, nothing happens. Then, very slowly, she lifts her arms. Above her head, two large boughs form a wide angle. With agonising precision, her arms make their shape, her body mimics the tree. She is wearing a pale green jumpsuit, a string of white beads around her neck. A red ribbon loops one ankle. She takes a few deep breaths, stretches and wiggles her fingers in a delicate way. She closes her eyes, finds her focus, then opens her eyes again.

The lines of muscle in her arms and shoulders are clearly defined. Her hair drifts about her face, soft and haphazard, a pleasing contrast to the rest. At a certain point – I hardly noticed it the first time I watched – some music starts playing. The background noise fades out and the crackle of the breeze is replaced by a tinkly piano and a haunting voice. There's no beat and no drum and no words, it's as if the music is connected to the position of her arms or the rhythm of her breathing; it emerges organically. She fixes her gaze on a point above the camera, chin poised, and the light falls down in a soft pattern, the shadows of leaves moving over her neck. Then she is perfectly still.

After a minute, the music swells and the video starts

playing at 6× speed, a little clock in the corner of the frame showing the seconds whizzing by. Clouds whirl and her hair moves in a frenzy. At 6.31 some of the higher branches start to whip back and forth; at 8.17 three birds land tentatively, then skitter off into the dulling sky. Very occasionally, you can see her chest rising and falling, but otherwise nothing moves. I did the maths. Factoring in the time-lapse, by the end of the fourteen-minute-long video, she has been holding the position for a little over an hour. I tried it myself one day, by an angular window, on the expensive yoga mat and looking down at the street below. After two minutes, my arms were in agony. The durational aspect of her performance is powerful. How can she bear that kind of pain? Perhaps this is why her followers find it easy to trust her – they understand her commitment. Several times, while watching her videos, I've found myself in tears. Of course, I know her, I know all about her; for a while she was my whole world, and when she left I felt bereaved. But I'm not alone, other people find her work moving, too. In a short time, she amassed a considerable audience, and she soon found that she had the power to make others see the world as she did: a difficult and stifling place.

Eight

While she refined her meditation technique, her physical regime went through several different phases, each more gruelling than the one before. For a few weeks, she focused on body weight exercises, things she could do without leaving the flat. I bought her a set of hand weights with a glazed bronze surface, like little sculptures, the kind of objects you longed to touch. When they arrived, the delivery man left them downstairs in the foyer, so I carried them up to the flat myself, one at a time. Days later, my back still twinged. While she did bicep curls and goblet squats, or one-armed planks with a gleaming weight held high in her free hand, I sat on the sofa with a heat patch pressed to my spine. She became rounded and firm, as though she'd grown a new kind of skin, a protective layer that covered her whole body. Suddenly, the weights were too small, they didn't challenge her anymore. I offered to buy new ones, but she shrugged ungratefully.

Her energy had shifted, she seemed stifled, cooped up. She needed to get out.

In January, she joined a gym. She even made a couple of friends. There was the lothario and there was the loner. She was sleeping with one or both of them, I wasn't sure. Often, when I came home, the flat was empty. I'd wander around, collecting the things she'd left behind. If there were dishes in the sink, I washed them. If a towel had slipped onto the bathroom tiles, I hung it neatly on the rack. I monitored everything very carefully. When her shampoo ran low, I made more; when she finished a box of organic nutritional powders, I replaced it. I still enjoyed these small devotions, but not as much. When she had first moved in, they had felt meaningful, I had felt honoured to perform them, like a priestess making offerings to a deity. But time passed and the work decreased in value. She was no longer grateful, she withheld her affections, and without this enchantment it was not much more than menial labour. I tried to approach the situation with a cool head. I didn't want to push her away.

When she went out, I didn't ask where she was going, or with whom. Occasionally, she dropped scraps of information, enough for me to piece together a vague picture of the things that now occupied her inner life. The two men were called Elliot and Simon. It was Elliot she was sleeping with; he was handsome, she said, and odd in a way that she enjoyed. On instinct, I hated Elliot, perhaps even more than I'd hated Paul. I'd never witnessed the start of her romance with Paul, but with Elliot I saw the glimmer of her early feelings, the flash of new desire, a twinge of something youthful and skittish that made me nauseous.

To feel her slipping away, to stand by and do nothing, required huge effort. I had no energy anymore. I barely ate, or I ate too much, I fell behind at work. My assistant, Tara-Louise, couldn't understand my inability to focus; her workload had become much greater now that she had to watch for my sloppy mistakes. I remembered how it had felt to live alone in the flat, the hollow quiet, the sterility, the mess; I remembered trying to write emails at work, seeing the words lose their grammar, drifting away from one another like pockets of warm air. I was scared to be alone, but it wasn't just that. Even virtually, without the smell or the feel of her, she has a power over the people who find her; once you've known her, it's hard to go back to a time before.

Nine

One morning, on my way to work, I stopped to look at the old coffee shop. A light was on inside, a shadow moving back and forth. The windows were newly frosted and the sign above the door had been painted over, though not yet replaced with anything else.

'It's reopening,' a voice said behind me. It was Paul, standing too close. He seemed taller than I remembered. He smelled clean and his hair was carefully arranged, he wore a crisp grey suit and a bright white shirt. In the dismal autumn light, for the first time I saw he was handsome, or that he could have been handsome if only something were slightly different – the line of his chin, or the way his hair parted – but then he moved, his expression shifted and the illusion crumbled. He looked average, sullen, tired. 'I need to talk to her,' he said.

'No,' I said quickly.

'It's not really up to you, is it,' he said.

His team were gathering at the entrance to our building, talking energetically – big gestures, nervous laughter. A lot of them were wearing trench coats, navy blue, or beige like mine. Their bags and briefcases might have been cut from the same leather as my own black bag. Paul was looking over at them, too. One of them waved. He turned back to me.

'I don't have time for this,' he said, as though I were the one who'd stopped to talk to him. Then, he started speaking too fast. His hands made strange, frantic movements. His whole face looked different, his eyes were cruel but there was something else in his expression – fear perhaps. He told me that her grandmother had died, and her mother had called him.

'Why would her mother call you?' I said.

'She wasn't answering her phone,' he said, then added: 'She didn't know we'd broken up.'

'You're lying,' I said.

He showed me the messages on his phone. It seemed unlikely that her mother would contact him if she knew what had happened. But it was possible that, not wanting to tell her mother what he'd done, she hadn't said anything at all.

I didn't know how to respond, I couldn't think fast enough. He checked his phone, briefly. Someone called his name and he stood taller. His suit really did look good.

'Maybe you're right,' he said, as though I had said something meaningful. 'It'll be nicer coming from you.'

I watched him join the group. I watched them all as they left the office behind.

It was difficult to know how to tell her, I had no idea how she might respond. I considered whether she might, in fact, prefer to hear it from Paul, who knew these people, who could share her bereavement in a way I could not.

'Paul was looking for you,' Tara-Louise said, when I arrived. 'Did he find you?'

I told her yes.

'He looked good in that suit, don't you think?' she said.

Later that day, when his team returned, Paul was flanked on all sides by colleagues recounting his triumphs, cheering and patting him on the back. He had cleared a man's name in a sexual assault case. 'You saved his life,' a young woman said, a new trainee. 'These days, in this climate, people don't recover from that kind of thing.'

They invited me to join them for drinks and I refused. Tara-Louise was tagging along. She was standing near Paul, the sides of their arms touching; she was laughing nervously at something he had said.

When I got home, the flat was empty, so I started making arancini – waiting for the rice to cream and then cool. She came home around seven and said she was already late, she was meeting Elliot, the guy from the gym, he was cooking some kind of special dinner, she had to go.

'You can't go,' I said.

'What?'

'I've got something to tell you,' I said.

'Well,' she said slowly. 'It can wait.'

I blurted it out. 'Your grandmother died.'

'Who?' she said.

'Your grandmother. She's dead. That's why your mother was calling you.'

She looked at her phone. 'How do you know?'

I explained the chain of communication – her mother and Paul, Paul and me. I wanted to tell her how, for a moment, I had really liked his face, that I had finally understood, in a glimpse, what she had seen in him all along. She sat down then stood up again.

'Why Paul?' she said.

'I suppose she didn't know what else to do.'

The arancini were still frying. From time to time, the oil sparked and burned the back of my hand. She paced the length of the dining table a few times, then, with hands lightly trembling, picked up her phone and called her mother.

I opened a bottle of wine, poured two large glasses and drank half of mine in one go. The other glass, I took to her.

'Not now,' she said, batting me away. 'So what will we do?' she said to her mother, unsympathetic and practical.

I put dishes on the table – salads, breads, cheeses.

She hung up. She slapped a hand against the window and for a moment my heart stilled, fearing that, given the size of her biceps, the glass would break, leaving nothing between her and the tarmac below.

She moved away. I poured more wine into her untouched glass, filling it almost to the brim. She sat down.

I asked how her mother had sounded on the phone.

'I still don't know why she called Paul,' she replied. 'She didn't even like him.' She downed her glass and filled it again.

'Did you ask her?' I said.

'No.'

'Why didn't you just answer your phone?' I said.

'Why are you taking her side?'

'I'm not,' I said.

'I don't know why she couldn't have just waited,' she said. 'I would have called her eventually.' She pouted her lips and glared like a teenager.

I tipped the arancini into a bowl, forgetting to pat them dry. The excess oil formed an orange pool. She came and stood next to me; her body was warm against mine, her breath smelled sweet.

Suddenly, she looked furious. 'I've never even met my grandmother,' she said.

I asked her to explain.

She ate a couple of arancini and made a face. 'Too greasy,' she said, wiping her hands on a dishcloth. 'I mean, my mother never spoke to her mother, my grandmother didn't even know about me.' She picked up the dish of arancini and tipped the lot into the bin.

'God forbid that someone doesn't know about you,' I said quietly.

She looked at me, surprised.

I immediately regretted it. I started to apologise, tears filled my eyes. I had hurt her, I thought. She was vulnerable and I had been cruel, but then she smiled as though delighted.

'Don't worry, Susie,' she said sweetly. 'It's good to say what you think.'

She told me she was going to Elliot's for the night. After that, she said, she would find her own place to live.

Ten

The next morning, I toasted hazelnuts for her muesli and brewed coffee in the Turkish pot, before I remembered she wasn't there. I ate the muesli myself. I drank the whole pot of coffee. A knot came together in the middle of my body – a lump of something dark and unpleasant that shifted from my stomach to my throat. I imagined the muesli curdling as it made its way down; I wondered if coffee could congeal. I thought of the medieval humours we had learned about in school: blood, yellow bile, black bile, phlegm. I pictured the inside of my body as merging rivers of black and yellow sludge.

I called Tara-Louise and told her to reschedule my appointments for the day.

'Are you ill?' she said.

'Yes, that's correct.'

'You don't sound ill, you sound fine.'

'It's not that kind of illness, is it,' I said.

'You need a mental health day, is that it?'

'No,' I said. I coughed loudly several times.

'Okay,' she said. 'I get it, you're ill.'

I left the flat and walked quickly, without knowing where I was going. The weather was unusually warm. People were taking off their coats, draping them over their arms, everyone in a rush, everyone looking overburdened and hot. So much of being an adult is just carrying things around, I thought: coats, shopping, bags, computers, charging leads, spare pairs of shoes. I kept waiting for the day that my life was finally in order, when I would have one small bag containing everything I needed, so that when I entered a room people would think: she's free, she's made it. I walked to the railway station and considered my options. I wished I had a car – it was possible to drive in an angry way but harder to exercise your emotions on public transport. A list of potential destinations flicked by on the screens overhead. I could go to York or Manchester, I could go to the coast and take a long walk. In the end, I took the shortest journey possible, to a nearby shopping complex with a cinema and a food court and the kind of artificial lighting that gave me a headache.

The train carriage was full of mothers with pushchairs and prams. Mostly, the babies were sleeping, but a few cried and mewed. Their sounds were so tender and direct, it was painful for me to hear them. At what point did children learn to keep their feelings to themselves? I pressed my earphones further in and played the noisiest song I could find. A small boy stood in the aisle by my seat and looked at me. I smiled at him, but he just kept looking as though he were waiting for an answer to a question, so I turned away and pretended I hadn't seen him, as if he wasn't real.

When the train pulled in, it was raining hard. I tried to run but my skirt was restrictive, my skin was hot and itching all over. I tore off my jacket and threw it in the bin. It felt good to be wasteful; I wondered what else I could throw away. The first shop I came to sold the kind of sportswear that was no good for sport. Music blared from free-standing speakers, the lights were too bright for comfort, the floor was shiny and slippery, recently polished, pale blue. Behind the till, a cashier was picking sleep from her eyes. The clothes were made from luxurious, impractical materials, satin, velour and lace. They were expensive and casual, a combination I had never understood before. I bought a purple velvet tracksuit and some gold trainers with a wedge heel. The whole outfit came to two hundred and fifty-seven pounds. It felt good to spend money on nothing, to feel like money didn't mean anything, like I was just getting rid of it, washing it away. I changed in the toilets, I put my blue skirt and blouse in the carrier bag. Immediately, I felt much better, like someone else.

Further inside the shopping centre, there was a department store. The light there was yellow and warm. Even before I'd gone in, several people in uniforms smiled at me. It felt like heaven not to be at work, to be here where I was so important. I trawled the various beauty counters, testing lipsticks and powders on the back of my hand. Everywhere smelled of talc and lilies, apart from a table full of colognes which smelled chemical, like glass polish or engine coolant. The counters were glossy and slick and dark. When an assistant approached and asked if there was anything I wanted to try, I told her that I wanted to look like somebody else.

'A celebrity?' she asked.

'Not necessarily.'

'Or like someone you know?'

'Whatever you like,' I said.

Her face seemed to be made of dust, the surface was chalky and dry. She had painted over her eyebrows in concealer and drawn them on again higher up her face.

'We have a new kit this month,' she said, and rattled through a large drawer before pulling out a black case the size of a laptop. 'This has literally everything you need, for whatever you want.'

I stared at her.

'You're right,' she said. 'It's overwhelming.' She showed me a series of pictures, one woman made to look like ten. The room was so bright and the pictures so glossy, all I could see were a few dark lines and the reflected glare of the electric lights above. I pointed at random.

'That one,' I said.

I took off my glasses and sat down. The world around me softened and blurred.

First she wiped my face with a sweet-smelling lotion and washed it off with a warm flannel, then she applied various creams and gels and finally powders over my skin. It was meditative, just sitting there, a blank space for someone to fill. It was curious to me that it was socially acceptable for a stranger to be touching me for so long. No one had helped me into the new clothes I'd bought. If I wanted to buy a new toothbrush, would somebody brush my teeth?

'Do you usually wear bronzer?' she said.

I told her no.

'Highlighter? Powder? Fixing spray?'

No, no and no.

She laughed and it sounded cruel.

The whole thing took a long time, all the touching and dabbing and blending. I imagined myself like a lump of clay – she would decide my final form. When at last the assistant showed me my face in the mirror, I could hardly see myself. There were grey and white stripes on my cheeks, my lips were three different colours. Parts of my face were so shiny they appeared to have been dipped in platinum, while other parts were so caked in powder it seemed they might crumble and fall off.

'We went for an ombré lip,' the assistant said, not to me but to one of her colleagues. 'And a pewter metallic eye.'

'Gorgeous,' the colleague said. 'Would you like us to take a picture of you?'

I declined, but the assistant took a selfie with me anyway. 'I'm trying to go freelance,' she said, pulling a cotton bud from behind a mirror and wiping it gently beneath my eyes. I realised the experience was over and that I would be left alone again. A feeling of panic seized my chest. 'Would you like to take anything home with you today?' she said. 'Or I could write it all down for you?'

I looked again in the mirror. My eyelids were dark and gleaming. My skin was pale and pearlescent, an entirely foreign surface. The assistant pulled out a notepad in the shape of a face. She formed big round letters over the eyes, cheeks and lips. All the products had industrial names. *Eyebrow pencil in Pit Brow Lasses. Highlighting stick in Davy Lamp.* I bought the eye pencil. The shade was *Bituminous Kohl.* It looked like a wax crayon and cost thirty-five pounds. She dropped a miniature lipstick and a tester for face cream into the bag, she smiled so hard at me I wanted badly to give her a hug. I told her I'd take the highlighter as well, and she gave me a sachet of perfume. I walked away quickly, afraid of myself.

The shopping centre glowed beneath the artificial light. There were children everywhere. I fished around in my handbag and pushed the earphones back into my ears. I found a playlist I recognised from childhood, violent songs my brothers used to play. The new trainers were springy and made me walk with a little bounce, they squeaked against the freshly mopped floor. Guitars thrashed through the headphones, a man screamed and I broke into a skip. The whole place was designed to disorientate so I let myself get lost, surfing escalators and turning corners without thinking. At one point I stopped to look at a green faux-fur coat in an expensive-looking window display. Behind the coat, small mirrors hung from the ceiling at different heights. They reflected back at me dissected portions of my face. I stood there, admiring the assistant's handiwork, the way she'd made it seem like I was emitting my own light, and when I moved away again I felt depleted, the energy of the whole experience, the intimate encounter with another person already slipping away. I bought three cans of gin and tonic from a supermarket concession. I opened one and sipped as I walked. From time to time, I pulled out my phone and took a picture of myself. The make-up made me ageless – I might have been eighteen or fifty-five. When the cans were gone, I found I was hungry so I walked to the food court and ordered a bucket of fried chicken with a side of nachos and a side of fries. I shoved the polystyrene containers into the carrier bag with my discarded work clothes and smuggled the whole lot into the cinema.

The only films showing at eleven thirty in the morning were for kids. I chose one about two teenage girls who became witches at boarding school. When I pulled out my boxes of food, the mums sitting near me turned to glare. One by one, I pushed greasy lumps of chicken into my mouth. It tasted of nothing; even the chilli was bland. I'd become so used to my wholesome and organic dinners that junk food was now an alien substance my taste buds refused. Still, the shovelling action was a comfort; chewing, it turns out, is good for the soul.

The film was funny in places, but mostly absurd. The two girls were played by women in their late twenties, while their mothers looked to be in their early thirties. When they all had boyfriends, they were happy; when they had none, they were sad. I sensed some real affection in the relationship between the two lead actresses, something that couldn't be performed and belonged to their off-screen lives. In the scenes where they were supposed to be 'bad witches', they flirted with one another outrageously. I fantasised about the filmset. Had their trailers been close together? Had they swapped clothes and beauty products and stayed up late like the characters in the film? At the end of the story, when the two girls had to return to their provincial, upper-class homes, I sobbed loudly while the mums looked on dismayed.

I bought four more cans of gin and tonic for the train home. I drank two on the journey, and the other two between the station and the flat. When I arrived at the flat, I paused with my key in the lock. Behind the door were various futures. She would be there, packing up her things; she'd be so glad to see me she'd decide to stay. She would be there, not packing, having already decided not to leave. She wouldn't be there, because she hadn't come back yet, or because she had already packed and left. I went in. There was no one at home and her things were still there.

I was sick – first the chicken and fries, then a wash of gin and bile. I wiped the toilet bowl clean and stood up and caught my reflection in the mirror. The metallic grey eyeshadow had run down my cheeks in hard lines. I must have rubbed my eyes while I was eating because some of it was smeared around my mouth. The foundation on my nose was flaking and my lips were ashen pale with a dark purple line at the edges. For a moment, I laughed, but the way my face moved under the make-up, the way my skin appeared to crease, was so horrifying that quickly I stopped. There was a bottle of almond oil in her washbag. I poured it into a cupped palm and worked it over my skin until it formed a slick. I watched myself become subterranean, something dredged up from the slime, then I washed and washed my face. Beneath the make-up, the skin was hectic and uneven, red in patches and peeling. When I looked up again, I saw I'd broken a blood vessel in one eye.

From the dining table, my phone made an awful rattling sound. It was Tara-Louise. 'What is it?' I said. 'I'm off sick.'

'Yes, I know,' she said. 'There's a complication with the Jameson case.'

'I'm not dealing with that today,' I said. 'You do it.'

'I can't.'

'Listen,' I said. My voice had become hard, as if something had seized me around the throat. My neck was hot, my palms were sweating. I didn't have anything specific to say, just a mad and desperate feeling that, somehow, I wished to communicate.

'Susie?' she said. 'Are you there?'

'I'm going to be sick,' I said, and hung up. I switched off the phone, threw it in with the kitchen utensils and slammed the drawer shut.

The light in the apartment was glorious, as it often is in the afternoon. The sun had tipped past its midpoint and dropped into view over the industrial skyline. It warmed the thick glass in the windows and made wide pools on the floor.

I stood on her yoga mat. I raised my arms above my head and reached up. I felt queasy again and sat down, but then I thought, no: if she can be peaceful, so can I.

Her laptop was open on the kitchen table. At the click of a button, the screen came to life. There were a great many tabs in the browser – guided meditations, sea life sounds, detailed diagrams of leaves, articles on the somatic body and layers of consciousness. I searched *yoga* in her browsing history, and a huge list of links appeared. I chose one at random.

A fresh-faced thin white American woman appeared on the screen. Her yoga mat was positioned between some nice-looking plants. A happy little dog ran about between her legs and, while she was explaining the purpose of the video, she stopped from time to time to scratch it under the chin. *Today, we're going to be opening our hips,* she said. *This requires us to be kind to ourselves.* I removed my new trainers and the tracksuit jacket. I pulled my hair into a ponytail. The woman looked so kind, I wished she were really in the room. I wished she could show me how to position my legs correctly, how to straighten my body, how to look long and elegant.

Stand at the top of your mat, the nice American woman was saying. *Plant your feet down. Move your ears away from your shoulders. Keep your neck long and your head tall.* My feet stayed where they were, my ears and shoulders remained the same distance apart. I tried stretching my neck long but it sent a shooting pain down my back. *Activate the arches of the feet. Spread the toes.* The very idea of spreading toes made me feel extremely unwell. *If you need to stop at any point,* she said, *just come into child's pose and reconnect with the breath.*

I made it through the first fifteen minutes, lurching clumsily from one posture to the next, doing my best not to collide with the steel dining table and crack my head open. In the windows, I could see a faint reflection of myself. It was off-putting, I had none of her strength, none of her poise. *Breathe into the back body,* the American lady said, but my lungs didn't seem to have a front or back. When she said to *bend forward and nudge the shoulders behind the knees,* I gave up. I couldn't remember what child's pose was and so I just tipped myself onto one side. I lay there with my limbs splayed, like someone who'd fallen out of a plane and, when I couldn't stand the sound of her voice any longer, I slammed the laptop shut.

When she came to pack her things, she didn't seem surprised to find me there in the flat. She made no comment about my face and clothes. I thought she might have something to say about the state of the apartment – the breakfast materials strewn over the table, the work clothes I'd chucked in the kitchen sink – but she said nothing. She was wearing some ugly shorts I'd never seen her in before, and football socks. She clearly hadn't showered, her hair was plastered to her head, her roll-neck top was damp with sweat. She walked over to one of the windows and looked out over the city. The evening light was pink and grey, there was rain on the horizon, a dark blue smudge.

Slowly, gracelessly, I stood up.

'How are you?' I said.

She looked at me. She was distant, preoccupied. She walked around the flat as if she'd never seen it before. There had been a time when I'd imagined her moving out and how she'd thank me for all that I'd done. She'd put her arms around me and her breath on my neck as she explained to me how I'd nursed her back to health, lifted her out of depression, helped to rebuild her life. In reality, she hardly looked at me. She took everything I had bought for her – the yoga mat, the tea paraphernalia, the oils and tinctures from the bathroom, the nicer of the two pot plants – and was gone.

There were three bottles of wine in the fridge. I drank one and passed out on the sofa. When I woke up, it was late and I was in bed, still wearing the velour tracksuit bottoms. Briefly, I wondered if I had put myself to bed or if she had forgotten something and come back and carried me there, one final moment of tenderness between us.

Eleven

That weekend, I called Tara-Louise. I hadn't planned quite what to say, but Tara-Louise seemed so well adjusted, I thought that she could probably afford to do favours for people she didn't really like. 'Look,' I began nervously. 'Are you doing anything tonight?'

'Of course I am,' she said. 'But it isn't more work, if that's what you've got in mind.'

'No,' I said, and paused.

'Then what? Are you still unwell?'

'Is it the kind of thing I could do with you?' I asked.

'How do you mean?' She sounded suspicious.

'I've been going through something,' I told her. 'I would prefer not to be on my own.'

Reluctantly, she gave me the name of the bar where she'd arranged to meet her friends. I was about to hang up when she said: 'Susie? I know you're my boss and everything, but please don't embarrass me tonight.'

The bar itself was complicated. We all bought top-up cards and then chose our wines from vending machines. For the first hour, that was all we talked about – how to pay for the wine, how to work the machines. There were eight of us around the table and the place was loud, so most of the time I could only guess at what the others had to say. I smiled a lot, I hardly said anything myself. When the cheeseboard arrived, I cut pieces for everyone. I passed the chutney and refilled the water glasses. I laughed at jokes I didn't under-stand. I concentrated hard to follow winding anecdotes about weddings I hadn't attended, I agreed that several films I'd never seen were very bad. There was a woman named Jodie and a man named Charles; they kept touching one another's knees.

'How long have you been together?' I asked them when a conversation came to a lull.

'We're brother and sister,' Jodie said calmly.

'But don't worry,' said Charles. 'We get that a lot.'

I smiled harder, nodded furiously. I offered to buy every-body a drink on my top-up card, but it turned out I hadn't put enough money on it and the whole thing took a very long time.

At the end of the night, Tara-Louise took me to one side. We were standing outside the bar, her friends were ordering taxis, I was trying to remember the late-night bus routes. She put a hand on my arm. She was drunk. She whispered loudly: 'Can I tell you something, Susie?'

'Okay,' I said. I thought she was going to tell me that it was awkward for her, having me spending time with her friends, it wasn't part of her job, I had overstepped the mark.

'You're nice,' she said. 'I didn't know.'

I gave her a hug, she kept her arm around me.

'You know, I don't really like any of them,' she said. 'Especially Charles.'

Charles turned to look at us. Tara-Louise seemed not to notice. My whole body felt hot. I remembered being at school, when it was normal to be with other people all the time, when we all hated the same things.

I didn't sleep that night. I sat on the floor where the yoga mat had been. A new bar had opened at the end of my road. I watched drunk people stagger along the street below. When a woman stopped to be sick in a drain, I put on my jacket and shoes. I'd take her some water, I thought, I'd make sure she was all right, but then her friends caught up with her. They were a nice-looking group with well-made coats, deep pockets, plush scarves in jewel colours. A man with a good jawline helped her up. I took off my jacket and sat down again. I spent an hour or so reading self-help blogs. *How to deal with sad thoughts*. A lot of the advice seemed to rely upon startling imagery. *If you think a bad thought, just throw it away! Imagine it's a little paper bird. Catch it in your hand, then screw it up and throw it in the bin.* I wanted something practical, something that would tell me what to do. Eventually I found it. *Plan everything*, it said. *Account for every moment of your time.*

Twelve

On Sundays, I made meals for the week ahead. I planned to watch movies, sometimes two in one night; I planned to read a chapter or two chapters or fifty pages of my book. I started reading philosophical things, they demanded a different kind of attention. Often, I'd get to the end of a paragraph and have to go back to the beginning again, sometimes reading the same sentence ten times over. Some people might have found this off-putting, but to me it just seemed efficient: if, in the time I set out to read twenty pages, I only read one page, then I wouldn't have to find some other activity later on. I read slowly, I thought slowly, I was becoming more thoughtful about everything I did. If my shower didn't take the full twelve minutes I'd allotted, I'd fill the time in some other way, bookmarking philosophy lectures, or trying to draw an impossible shape. At night, if I couldn't sleep, I just said the word *sleep* in my head on repeat because that's what I'd written in the plan. *Sleep, sleep, sleep,* I'd say to myself silently, until eventually I'd wake up and see eight hours had passed.

I worked hard. For a while, I came home from work and felt, every day, that this was how it would be: work and then home, the empty flat and whatever happened to end it all, an accident, some kind of fall, then dying alone in an open-plan dining area with experimental windows. I carried on. The flat continued to feel empty, I continued to stick to the plan. I increased my mortgage payments. I lived sensibly, within my means. I didn't know what it all meant, perhaps nothing.

It was Tara-Louise who first told me about her videos. One of the other assistants had found them and shared the link. I watched them all, one after the other, her strange meditations. Sometimes she would be sitting or lying down, but there was always some part of her body that reflected a natural line, either a branch or some curvature in the earth or the border of the hedgerow in the background. If she was filming indoors, there would be a painting or a bright swathe of silk for her to work around. She would manoeuvre herself into some simple but beautiful arrangement, breathe deeply, settle into her task, and then the music would begin, and I would be carried away by her stillness, her strange talent for staying in one place. She must have accelerated her training programme because in each new video she was stronger again. Her arms were heavily sculpted, her legs broad pillars of muscle. She seemed to be growing all over now – her hands were vast, her wrists thicker. Somehow, I could not guess how, she had built muscle in her neck. And even where there was no muscle, she had expanded. There was more volume in her hair, her lips were fuller than before.

Sometimes, Tara-Louise and I watched the videos together, at lunch. Tara-Louise would ask if I'd heard from her, and I would say no and feel something like shame. But one evening, I looked at my phone and saw that I'd missed a call. I hadn't heard the phone ring, perhaps it had only rung for a second. When I called her back, she didn't answer. It must have been an accident, I told myself. She didn't really want to talk to me. But even as these thoughts arose, I was already thinking about what to cook for her when she returned, the new things she might like, all the ways I could help her with her work. I called her back, still nothing. Then late at night, as I was getting into bed, I saw her name appear on my phone. I answered so quickly, it didn't even ring.

Our conversation was brief. She wasn't moving back in, she didn't have a lot to say, but there was one last thing she wanted from me. I was to go to her old house in the suburbs to pick up the last of her things. Paul would be there, waiting for me.

Thirteen

On the day of the collection, I ran into Paul in the break room. He confirmed the arrangements with me, he spooned sugar into his coffee. He smiled a half-smile as he said: 'It's all packed and ready to go. I don't know why she can't just come and get it herself.'

When Tara-Louise asked me what was wrong, why I was so distracted that day, I explained what I had to do.

'Is that so bad?' she said.

'Paul wasn't good to her,' I explained. I didn't know if she'd believe me; Paul was popular at work.

'Text me,' she said quickly. 'When you get home.'

Paul answered the door and greeted me warmly, as though we were old friends. It was strange to go back to their house; I couldn't remember my last visit. Had there been paintings she'd wanted to show me? I looked around, there were no paintings now, but still it all felt oddly familiar, as though she'd only just left, or as though she might walk in at any moment. There were pictures of her everywhere, on the fridge, in small frames on the table, on the walls: her and Paul on holiday, her as a child with her mother. It was the end of July; ten months had passed since they had broken up. It was as if she existed on a different timeline to the rest of us: her whole life was different, she had a whole new career, her body was transformed. It seemed to me that Paul and I were the same people we'd always been, or if anything, we'd regressed.

Paul's manner was different outside the office. I only knew him in a suit, but here he was in comfortable trousers, a dirty T-shirt, hair scruffy and wearing glasses. He seemed a little nervous, entirely unthreatening. His movements were gentle. Without asking me if I wanted one, he handed

me a cup of tea, having made it as I prefer it, brewed strong with a splash of milk and one heaped sugar. He offered biscuits and I took one, without thinking. I tried to remember what she had said to me about him, to picture what he had done.

'Are you all right?' he asked.

'I'm fine,' I told him. 'I'm really just here to get her stuff.'

'We've known each other a long time, Susie,' he said. 'We have a history too.' He made his mouth into a placatory line and tilted his head to one side.

The smell of hot, sweet tea drifted upwards and mingled with something else. Perhaps the bins needed taking out, there was a pile of recycling by the back door. I told him I needed to use the loo. My chair made an uncomfortably loud noise as it scraped over the kitchen tiles. In the hallway, I tripped on a step.

'Watch yourself, Susie,' he said.

The upstairs bathroom had an awkward sliding door. I fumbled with it and realised my hands were shaking. Inside, it smelled strongly of aftershave, like leather and smoke. Dregs of shaving foam and stubble remained in the basin. I looked at myself in the mirror and thought of her looking at herself in the mirror. I decided I wanted to see the box room, to see where she had slept all those nights. I wondered if the objects she had hidden were still there, or if he had found them and cleared them away: the headphones, the books, the pillow, the blanket, the toothbrush, the bottled water, the face wipes. I crossed the landing, the other rooms were all open, a spare bedroom with a large wall-hanging, the main bedroom with vast windows and a Victorian ceiling rose. Only one door was closed. I let my hand rest on the doorknob a moment. I was about to turn it when I heard Paul moving below.

'Are you all right up there, Susie?' he called.

Slowly, I made my way back down the stairs.

I didn't sit down again and nor did he. 'She told me what you did,' I said.

'Break-ups are complicated,' he replied.

'She said you used to lock her up.'

'I never forced her to do anything,' he said.

He said he understood that I would take her side, but that he wanted me to know that he had never laid a finger on her, had never so much as caused her to break a nail, whatever she might have claimed. He said their relationship had been unconventional and that she had been *troubled*, he had tried to persuade her to *seek help* but she had resisted, preferring to deal with things *in her own way*. This involved protracted periods of withdrawal and isolation where she would no longer engage in conversation. All she had wanted was to write in her journals, to be *in her own head*. She was selfish, uncaring; probably it had something to do with her mother. The sudden shifts in her personality, he said, had been very hard on him. For a long time, he had felt alone. He had not wanted the relationship to end, but that now it was over a small part of him was relieved: he no longer had to experience her daily rejection of him. Though, of course, he still missed her – there were tears in his eyes as he spoke. What they'd had was very special, he didn't expect he would ever feel the same way about anyone else.

Perhaps he had prepared for this moment, taking parts of her character he knew I would recognise and repurposing them to suit his needs. It was more likely, I thought, that he had not wanted to prepare, knowing that he would get a kick out of thinking on his feet. I supposed that he would feel very pleased with himself, after I had gone, for giving such a slick performance. I felt awful for having allowed him the satisfaction.

My throat was dry, and I didn't trust my voice, so I let him continue to talk. I ought to have silenced him, to have talked over him, to have told him I saw through him completely. Instead, I asked him where her things were stored and he led me into the living room, then he helped me to carry two large cardboard boxes and a plastic crate into the garden. I ordered a taxi. He stood and waited in the doorway. When the car arrived, he told the driver that to get to my flat at that time of day it was best to go the long way round. I looked back at him.

'How do you know that?' I said.

He smiled at me again, then he went back inside.

The traffic was bad. It started to rain. I took off my glasses; the outside world was a blur of water and movement and red, flashing brake lights. I closed my eyes for a moment to listen to the weather and the swish of tyres, then opened them again.

'Are you all right?' the driver asked, turning round to look at me. I nodded and swallowed and searched my bag for a headache pill.

I took the boxes up to my apartment. I sent a text to Tara-Louise. I told her I was fine, and it was true. Something had happened in that conversation with Paul, or while I'd been standing outside the tiny room at the end of the landing, or when I'd forgotten all my words and failed to defend her. I'd felt deeply ashamed, and a little space had opened up as a result. I remembered all the injustices that had been done to her, the humiliations she had suffered, the fact that she still couldn't bear to see him, and she made sense to me again. I poured myself a glass of water, took off my make-up, changed my clothes. *All she wanted to do was write in her journals*, he had said. Well, there they were, her notebooks, packed neatly into a crate.

Fourteen

Before I read the journals, I watched her videos again. Each one had a title like a painting. *Still Life with Pink Cloud, Still Life with Japonicus Plant.* In the description boxes, she linked to her other products – guided meditations and scented candles that could be purchased from her website. When I'd finished watching the most recent video, I poured a glass of wine and placed the notebooks on the dining table. A lot of them were from her time at university – they were mostly disorganised lecture notes, angry letters she'd written to her mother and never sent. There was a gap in time, when she had started at the firm, where she appeared not to have written a journal, or perhaps it had been misplaced or destroyed. Over the course of her relationship with Paul, she had only filled two notebooks, one large and green, the other small and pink.

I opened the green journal and started to read. The first page was dated like a diary entry, but what followed was an odd fable about a girl and a plant. The girl was sent to the shop. Upon arrival, she wasn't sure which kind of plant she ought to get – her mother had clear ideas, but she had forgotten what they were. In the end she was drawn to the widest, stateliest specimen. 'This one is very expensive,' the shopkeeper said. 'I should hope so,' she said. 'Because it is so good.' She paid for the plant. 'Be careful with it,' the shopkeeper said. 'They say it is possessed of a vigorous spirit.' The story continued over several pages. Eventually the girl and the plant became one. There was no mention of Paul, or anything I recognised from her life. Another story followed: The girl needed a pear for a delicious recipe, her grandmother used to grow pears but she couldn't remember where they had gone. What had happened to the pear tree? Was the house still there? She went to the library and found some instructions for growing a pear tree in only a week. All she needed was a patch of earth, a sigil, some sweet sherry, an HB pencil, a box of matches and a decent trowel. Eventually the pear tree tore down the village, its roots were so sprawling, its fruit so plentiful. The notebook was filled with these fables, uncanny stories of self-destruction. I read the whole lot in one sitting; there were many variations on similar themes. The girl wanted to cast a spell and had to source the ingredients from within her own body. The girl dug shallow graves and deep ones, she wriggled into the muddy banks of nearby rivers, swam into sinkholes, barricaded herself into natural caves, or carved vast tunnels into wet, cold sand. The ending was always the same – the girl was destroyed, and the girl emerged in a new form. I thought of her in the box room, trapped and alone, coming up with fantastical modes of escape. This was the account of her trauma, but it too had taken a different form. The smaller, pink notebook was full of strange symbols, shapes and lines arranged together but not in a way that made any sense to me. I wondered if it was some kind of mindfulness exercise, or if she had invented her own code. On a few pages, the symbols had been crossed out violently with heavy black biro. A lot of pages were missing, too. I slept terribly that night. I woke up many times. In my shallow sleep, I had disturbing dreams.

Fifteen

A few days later, she called to tell me she was ready to receive her things. She had already booked me a taxi and decided which train I would take back to Sheffield, she had bought me a ticket for the 14.06.

The cottage was in a grim little village, just off the A19. A lot of the houses there were empty, in various states of disrepair. There was a row of shops, all boarded up, and some kind of industrial facility with an austere metal fence. The taxi driver helped me to pile up the boxes at the front gate, and I gave him a large tip. When, eventually, she came to let me in she had two envelopes of cash in her hand, one for the driver and one for me.

'You don't have to pay me,' I said. 'I'm your friend.'

She insisted on giving me the money for the taxi, then she said, 'I don't have visitors anymore. This is strange.'

'It's nice to see you,' I told her. I looked around. The house was smaller than I had imagined, and darker. It needed repainting, the ceilings were cracked.

She made me a coffee and poured herself a green juice. She opened several cupboards and eventually produced a packet of biscuits, offering them to me without taking any herself. 'I mostly eat raw things now,' she told me.

'Like sashimi?'

'Eggs,' she said. 'Expensive ones. And plant-based foods.'

'Vegetables,' I said.

She said: 'Yes.'

A black mould laced the walls of the kitchen, the whole place felt damp. It didn't seem like the kind of place you would go in order to reinvent yourself; it seemed like somewhere you would go to give up completely.

'Are you happy here?' I asked her.

'It allows me to do what I want,' she replied.

In spite of her gloomy surroundings, she looked incredible, even better than the videos suggested: her skin was perfect and her hair gleamed. She really did seem to have an *inner stillness* – even when she was moving, she did it slowly and purposefully, as though her actions were inspired by some greater design. From time to time, I tried to touch her – a hand on her back, a tap on the arm. I helped to carry one of the boxes into the study.

'Did you read the journals?' she asked.

My heart skipped. 'Of course not,' I said. I gave her my best lawyer face.

She was smiling as she spoke. 'I don't care if you did.' Her eyes narrowed and her mouth became small. 'The past doesn't bother me anymore,' she said. 'I've learned to be free of it.'

I didn't know which parts of the past she was referring to, but she really did seem free. For the first time, I felt I was talking to a stranger. There were flashes of familiarity – a cadence in her speech, or the way her hands moved when she talked – but the balance had shifted. I had the sensation of meeting someone who reminded me of her. I almost wanted to tell her: you're just like someone I used to know.

'Don't you ever get lonely?' I asked. There was a lot of emotion in my voice, I could hear myself as though from a distance, as though listening to someone's child – rasping and plaintive, a pathetic little whine.

She drew nearer and looked down at me, as if I were a small animal – nothing too threatening, a vole or a mouse, something unwanted and pitiable.

'Poor Susie,' she said, and I thought I saw a flicker of something move across her face, a

tiny shadow of recognition. 'No,' she said. 'You don't have to worry about me anymore.'

Not long after that, she posted a video called *Still Life with Calathea*. In the description box, she suggested that we would all be better off on our own. It made solitude seem romantic; it appeared to suggest that if you would just give up the people in your life, then you could be beautiful and strong like her. It got a lot of attention from new viewers, it was shared widely, far beyond her usual audience. Overnight, she acquired thousands of new followers across her various platforms. For a while, her website was taken offline and when it returned it was brighter and slicker and easier to shop. Some people found her ideas confronting – they didn't want to live alone. They pointed to her as a symbol of everything that was wrong with the modern world, how it wanted us to compete, to prioritise self-interest, to live in ignorance of others' needs. The people who liked the video, however, often appeared to have good reason to want to be on their own. As they planned their new and isolated lives, they formed a different kind of community. Together, they calculated how much of civilisation they could afford to reject and how much it was necessary for them to keep. Later, when she posted more videos on the subject, some of their loved ones started showing up in the comments, too. They wanted to know: where were their children, their dear friends?

Sixteen

For a while, I stopped reading philosophy, I stopped worrying about work. I gave all my attention to her videos and the network of comments beneath. Many people had disappeared. I considered the details of their lives. What had made them so desperate to isolate themselves? I felt as though I had spent my whole life trying to narrow the distance between myself and others, trying to belong to the world they shared, to understand what they meant when they spoke.

I started thinking about the other people who had witnessed her transformation; as far as I knew it was only me and a couple of guys from the gym. I tried to remember what she had told me about Elliot – that he was reclusive, he hated his job, he talked to his mother a lot, he preferred the gym when it was quiet, in the early afternoons – so one Wednesday I took a late lunch break to see if he was there.

When I arrived, there was no one on reception and no one

in the gym either. A cleaner was washing the floor. I asked him if the gym was closed and he said no, but the changing rooms were also empty. In the cafeteria, two young mothers were having a chat while their babies slept in their prams, there was no one else. When I went back to reception, an extraordinarily good-looking man was leaning against the counter, playing on his phone.

'Hi,' I said.

He looked up. 'Hi.'

'Are you Elliot?' I asked.

'What?' he said. 'Elliot?'

'Yes, are you him?'

'Why is everyone looking for Elliot these days? Wait, you're not his girlfriend, are you? Because if you are, I hate to tell you, but he's literally never mentioned you before.'

'I'm not his girlfriend,' I said. 'If I was his girlfriend, hopefully I'd already know whether or not you were him.'

'Right, yeah,' the man said. 'Good point.' He seemed genuinely impressed. 'I'm Simon,' he said. 'Nice to meet you.' I knew about Simon, he had taught her some particular muscle-building technique, with a sandbag or a giant metal ball. She must have been sleeping with him too, I thought. He was so handsome, it was hard to focus, like looking directly at the sun.

'Is Elliot here? I'd like to talk to him.'

'No,' said Simon. 'We've not seen him for weeks.'

'He's left the gym?'

Simon shrugged. 'Sometimes he has a lot of work on,' he

said. 'Though someone else was here yesterday. His mother, she said. Said she hadn't heard from him in a while.'

I gave Simon my number and asked him to pass it on to Elliot if he ever came back, though I suspected he would not.

Seventeen

I decided to take some time out, I booked three weeks of annual leave. I had never been on holiday by myself before. I didn't know where I wanted to go. On my last day of work before the break, I asked Tara-Louise what she thought. 'If you could go anywhere on holiday, right now, tomorrow afternoon, where would you go?'

'Ibiza,' she said. 'The end of the season, the closing parties. You don't even have to get drunk. My friend Jodie was pregnant when we went. We all told her not to come, then she partied harder than anyone, she went out every single night.' She showed me a photograph on her phone, a small pregnant body silhouetted against the sunset.

From the promotional materials, it seemed that Ibiza was always either bathed in light or plunged into darkness, with nothing in between. There were glowing sunsets and sun-soaked hillsides. There were nightclubs with beaming, coloured lights; a DJ standing tall behind the decks like a priest before an altar. I booked the flights.

I packed light, I didn't have any of the right clothes, I'd have to buy new things when I got there. When I pictured myself on holiday, I imagined someone taller, broader, someone who might wear wide trousers or a sweeping, loose-fitting dress. At the airport, I walked slowly through the duty-free shops until someone at one of the beauty counters asked if I needed any help. I hadn't been wearing make-up recently, Tara-Louise said I looked better without it, but he applied some bronzer, a bright pink lipstick and some mascara. When he showed me my reflection, I looked cheerful and healthy, like a person who might be nice to talk to, like someone who doesn't worry so much. It was like looking at a version of myself from a parallel reality, where I felt good about my decisions, where I always knew what I wanted to say. He wrapped the products for me and wished me a pleasant trip.

In the lounge, I bought an apple juice and sat down to read. For once, I was able to concentrate, I read fifty pages of a large and difficult book, I understood it all. By the time the gate was called, I had reached the postscript, so I stopped at a bookshop on the way. I felt powerful, my mind was clear. There were no philosophy books, so I bought a self-help book about time management. Once we had boarded, the attendants told us that there had been delays and we would have to wait. They served sparkling water and onion-flavoured pretzels. The cabin was hot and dry. I finished the philosophy book, I had absorbed its message. I sat with my seat belt on, licking grains of onion salt from between my teeth.

The plane was two hours late, which didn't matter because nothing and nobody was waiting for me, I hadn't even booked a hotel. At the airport, I found a cash machine and took out some money. There was a taxi rank outside. I asked the driver to take me to a restaurant, somewhere near one of the clubs. There was a dusty garden courtyard. The waiters brought me a beer and a bowl of crisps. I ordered a dish from the specials board. Half an hour later, a plate of meat in tomato sauce arrived. I ate slowly. It was delicious to be sitting there in the evening light. From time to time, I came upon an olive, a little parcel of flavour, saline and wet.

A group of men came and sat at a table not far from mine. I could see them looking over. When I was halfway through the bowl of stew – it had already gone cold, but I didn't mind – one of the men came over to my table. He wanted to know where I was going that night and if I was planning to go there alone. I gave him the name of the club and he said he would be there with his friends, that we could share a taxi, they would buy me some drinks.

'I'm pregnant,' I told him. 'You don't have to drink to have a good time.'

He backed away.

Around ten thirty, I asked the waiter to call me a cab.

The club was empty. No DJs were playing yet. The people working the bar were applying lipstick in the mirrored glass behind the spirit shelf. In the ladies' toilets, I ripped open the cellophane packages from duty-free. The bronzer came with a free brush. I swept it over my cheeks. It was a pleasurable sensation. I applied it to my eyelids and my forehead, just as the assistant had told me to. The lipstick looked brighter somehow in the dark – a glorious, triumphant pink.

The music went on for hours. It was midnight, then two, then four o'clock. For a while, there was a video DJ playing footage of fairground rides. The sun came up and it was day-time again and still it wasn't time to go home. I danced and danced. At some point, the men from the restaurant found me, offering more drinks; I let them buy me a gin and tonic and drank half. I raised my arms above my head, my mind was perfectly empty, there was only noise.

When it was over, we were ushered outside, the crowd spilled onto the sun-soaked street. I watched people roll cig-arettes and joints and then I sat on the pavement and opened my book. I reread the first ten pages and then I put it away again. I got up and walked in one direction until the sun was well over the horizon. I was tired, but in a way that felt good. After a couple of hours, I came to a pastel-coloured hotel. I asked for a room.

'Do you want breakfast?' they said.

I said yes. I was shown to a beautiful table overlooking a kidney-shaped pool. There were eggs with hollandaise sauce, there was sliced cheese and apple tart. My room was on the top floor – capacious, a mountain view. I closed the shutters and took off my clothes, the sheets were cool and smooth. I slept for fifteen hours and then I went out dancing again.

Eighteen

I still watch her videos from time to time, they are still very beautiful. A few months ago, she was featured in one of the weekend supplements. Tara-Louise kept the magazine for me. The article gave a brief overview of her life – her isolated childhood, her career in law – and a résumé of the skills she'd had to acquire to create her channel: an online course in video editing, a digital marketing class. The interviewer had asked how much money she was making but she would only say that her videos were available for anyone to watch for free. There were photographs of the old stone house and the garden where she made her films. In one, you could glimpse the railway track and a train going by. A whole page of the magazine was given over to her portrait. Her hair was long, almost reaching her waist, and her forehead gleamed with sweat. Her clothes looked ridiculous on her body: meaningless concessions to conventional life. There were spots of light in her eyes, her mouth made an almost imperceptible smirk. She seemed both very young and very old: a spooky, wise child, a magical old woman from the woods.

Pictures of Elliot started to appear on the local news. For a long time, she was silent on the subject of her missing followers, but eventually she issued a statement, or rather, she posted a video of herself walking, impossibly slowly, from one end of the garden to the other. She had her back to the camera and was wearing a long white dress. It was uncomfortable to watch such effortful walking, it made my own limbs ache. In the description box, she wrote that it had come to her attention that one of her followers had made the brave decision to cut his loved ones out of his life. She said that she didn't know the details, she had not made contact with the man herself, but she had nothing but respect for anyone bold enough to break with their old way of living, to build a new future for themselves. In the immediate aftermath, she lost a lot of followers, but they were quickly replaced by newcomers, eager to know more about her anti-establishment lifestyle, to begin their own journeys towards selfhood and isolation. A few months ago, a podcast series was released in which she appears as a mysterious cult figure, preying on vulnerable internet users, brainwashing them into making dark and uncompromising choices about their lives. Perhaps they desire to inhabit a body so still and strong; perhaps they see her as someone who has learned to be unaffected by the rest of the world. That kind of immunity doesn't appeal to me. I like being anxious. It gives me a lot of energy, it helps me to see what's really important and what I might change. But her followers don't want change or flow or process, they want something permanent they can trust. Her aesthetic is consistent, so they fail to see that she is capricious, that like any god or archetype, she's as much yours as she is mine.

Acknowledgements

Thank you to Luke Kennard, Ruth Gilligan, Philip Langeskov, Priscilla Morris, Stephen Nashef and Eliza Robertson for reading early drafts and offering essential kindness and critique. A special thank you to Sharlene Teo for reading this book at the most crucial moment, and for our conversations, which are always inspiring to me. Thanks to the Arts Council for a grant to write a different novel, whose failure gave way to this one. Thank you to Laura Barber, Kiara Kent and Clio Seraphim, for caring for this book and its inhabitants so fiercely. Thank you to Niki Chang for being a wonderful editor and agent, and a generally brilliant person to know. Thank you to David Evans and Sophia Rahim for stepping in so gracefully. Thank you to Jenny Page for copy editing and encouragement. Thank you to Avni Doshi for responding so generously to this book, for making me feel suddenly glad to have written it after all. Thank you, Mike

James, for reading these chapters a hundred times, for your endless patience, for having faith in me always. Thank you to my mum for the most essential things, for laughter especially, and for sharing all this with my baby, too. Thank you to my dad for believing me capable of solving any problem, narrative or otherwise, for teaching me to find community and generosity in books, for everything. Thank you Kit, for joy.